D0402619

Margaret Pumphrey's
Pilgrim Stories

Margaret Pumphrey's
Pilgrim Stories

Revised and expanded
by Elvajean Hall

Maps by JON NIELSEN

AN
APPLE
PAPERBACK

SCHOLASTIC INC.
New York Toronto London Auckland Sydney

If you purchased this book without a cover you should be aware that this book is stolen property. It was reported as "unsold and destroyed" to the publisher and neither the author nor the publisher has received any payment for this "stripped book."

Pilgrim Stories is published with the approval and collaboration of Plimoth Plantation in Plymouth, Massachusetts. It is a revision and adaptation of Margaret Pumphrey's *Pilgrim Stories* expanded with additional incidents from Bradford's *Of Plimoth Plantation* and Mourt's *Relation*.

No part of this publication may be reproduced in whole or in part, or stored in a retrieval system, or transmitted in any form or by any means, electronic, mechanical, photocopying, recording, or otherwise, without written permission of the publisher. For information regarding permission, write to Scholastic Inc., 730 Broadway, New York, NY 10003. APPLE PAPERBACKS is a registered trademark of Scholastic Inc.

ISBN 0-590-45202-9

Copyright © 1991 by Rand McNally & Company. Copyright 1961 under International Copyright Union by Rand McNally & Company. All rights reserved. This edition is published by Scholastic Inc., by arrangement with Rand McNally & Company.

12 11 10 9 8 7 6 5 4   2 3 4 5 6/9

Printed in the U.S.A.   40

For my nieces and nephew,
LOUISE, MARGOT, and BUZZ HALL,
Descendants of John Alden
and Priscilla Mullins,
who came in the *Mayflower*
— E.H.

Contents

1.
Meeting in Secret

One June morning in 1606 twelve-year-old Jonathan Brewster and his little sister Patience were trying out a new boat on the fish pond. Behind them rose Scrooby Manor, once the home of a nobleman but now a rambling old inn of forty rooms, managed by their father, William Brewster.

Hardly had Jonathan's little boat touched the water when a distant sound made both children forget all about the toy. It was the long, clear note of a horn.

"The King's messenger!" shouted Jonathan.

Scrooby was one of the "stations" on the Great North Road in England, a place where the King's officers, hurrying with messages from the palace in London, could stop to rest and change horses on their way north.

Jonathan and Patience did not have long to wait.

A second call showed that the rider was well out of Sherwood Forest, the wood where Robin Hood and his merry men once lived. Soon a great, black stallion swept into sight. In the courtyard a stable boy grabbed for the horse's bridle as the rider leaped to the ground.

"Prepare for the Queen!" he announced. "Our most gracious Queen Anne and her party will rest here tonight."

"This is short notice to prepare for a royal guest, but we will do the best we can to make them welcome," Mrs. Brewster promised.

Many times during that afternoon the two Brewster children dashed to a window, thinking they heard the royal guest approaching. But the sun sank lower and lower and still no one came.

"Perhaps they have lost their way," whispered Patience.

"They have a guide," Jonathan assured her.

"Then maybe they have been killed by robbers!"

In those days many travelers were jumped on by robbers who beat them to death and took all they had. No wonder Patience was fearful that something had happened to the Queen. But before the sun had quite disappeared from sight, the far-away note of a horn brightened every worried face in Scrooby.

A few more moments of waiting and then over the bridge and into the manor yard swept a company of knights surrounding a coach.

As the door of the coach was opened, the cry rang out, "Long live the Queen!" News of the royal visit had spread and many people had gathered to get a glimpse of their Queen.

Jonathan waved and shouted with the rest, but little Patience was strangely silent. As she glanced from one to another of the women who stepped from the coach, her chin began to quiver. Queen Anne hadn't come after all; these were just four dusty, tired-looking women. Patience was hoping for a queen with jewels at her throat and a sparkling crown on her head — all studded with diamonds and rubies and pearls.

"Jonathan, what has happened to her? She didn't come," the child whispered, tugging at her brother's arm.

"Hush, silly," he ordered. "That's the Queen herself, the one in the blue gown. Queens don't wear their crowns when traveling."

Perhaps the Queen heard the two children, for she looked right at them and smiled.

It was hard that night to be bundled off to bed at the usual time. But Mrs. Brewster would grant no favors, as she believed children should be neither seen nor heard when guests were present.

Next morning Patience was up early. She dressed as quickly as a six-year-old could and slipped down to the garden to gather flowers for the breakfast table. Yet, early as she was, she found someone in the garden before her. Someone was bending over her own bush of red roses. It was the Queen!

Patience did her best to remember her manners and curtsied in the way her mother had taught her. Then she wondered what to do next. She wondered if she should back all the way into the house. She knew she must not turn and run; not even children were allowed to turn their backs on a queen.

Then Queen Anne seemed to sense her plight and said, "I am admiring your roses, little one. How fresh and pretty they are with the morning dew still on them."

"This bush is my very own." Patience chattered away as she began to relax and pick flowers. "I call these the Bradford roses because Will Bradford gave me the bush."

"And who is Will Bradford?"

"Oh, a boy from Austerfield near here. He is father's friend and comes over to services every Sabbath. We have our own chapel right here."

"Why, how strange," mused the Queen. "I noticed a very pretty little church as we rode through the village last evening. I should think you would all rather go there."

"That is the King's church," blurted out Patience. "If we go there, we have to worship just as the King wants us to, but father thinks the King's way is wrong. Lots of people in Scrooby say the King's way is wrong!"

"King James would not like to hear that," the Queen said gently. "And it would not be safe for you to talk so freely to every stranger."

Poor little Patience! What had she said? She clapped her hand over her mouth as she suddenly remembered that she was telling a very great secret. Her face turned as red as the roses she was holding, and her eyes filled with tears.

"Never mind, child," the Queen comforted her. "Your secret is safe with me."

The Brewsters and some of their neighbors continued to hold church services in Scrooby Manor. They were called *Separatists* because they wanted to separate from the Church of England. They wanted to go their own way and choose their own minister instead of having one sent to them by the King's bishop.

They wanted to read from the Bible and talk about the things they had read with their pastor. They were willing to have other people worship God according to their own beliefs; all they asked was to be allowed to do the same. But their way was against the laws of England, and they knew they would be punished if they were caught.

One day Jonathan Brewster came dashing down the road, his hair flying in the wind, yelling at the top of his voice for his father.

William Brewster, hearing all the racket outside, came to the Manor door.

"Father, Father!" gasped the winded boy.

"They've caught several men already and they're on their way to Scrooby for you!"

"Who? Quick boy, tell me. . . ." Jonathan's father listened carefully to his son's story. Then, after a minute, he shook his head and said under his breath, "I am afraid they have found out about our secret church services."

Turning quickly, he went into the house, Jonathan hard at his heels. In low tones he explained to his wife.

"The King's officers have always known that we are a God-fearing people. They have had spies watching us for some time, I fear. They knew that if we were not going to the King's church, we must be going somewhere. They have learned of our secret meetings here in Scrooby Manor and are on their way to arrest us."

"Oh, you must be joking; surely they will not arrest all of us just for praying to God and reading the Bible."

"Perhaps not you women and children," replied her husband. "But the men will be put in prison, so we must fly — and fly quickly!"

Turning to white-faced Jonathan, Brewster said, "Run as fast as your legs can carry you and warn our pastor. Somebody else must get through to Austerfield and tell young Bradford. He, too, is in danger. Somebody will have to see Cooke, Southworth, Morton, and the rest. We have still time to slip into Sherwood Forest if we hurry."

"Does everybody know where to go?"

"Yes, it has all been planned. Thank goodness soldiers are not likely to stop a twelve-year-old."

One by one, the men of Scrooby village and the nearby farms got the message and disappeared. The warning had come just in time. In a few hours officers were hunting here and there about the village. Some patrolled the road. Others just sat — hour after hour — watching the houses. After dark they peeped into windows.

For the next few weeks it was the children's job to watch the officers and report to their mothers where they were and when they had left. Then a few people could slip out of the village with food and clothing for the fathers hiding in the woods, and drop their little bundles here and there at spots marked along the road that ran through Sherwood Forest.

Weeks later when the King's officers had moved on, the men of Scrooby came home. They still held their secret church services, but they were more careful now. Each Sunday they met in a different place. Often the services were held at night, and they would approach the building one by one so that it would not look as if a group were meeting.

One night the pastor, John Robinson, was teaching up in the loft of a barn. He held his Bible close to his eyes because the moon gave the only light he had to read by. Suddenly voices were heard below.

"I'd swear I saw two men come into this barn," said one.

"And I'd swear I saw a woman and two children disappear around the corner not a minute ago," said another. "If there were even a speck of light here, I'd say a secret meeting were being held! Shall we prowl around a bit and find out?"

Up in the loft each of the handful of men, women, and children held their breath. Finally the searchers below decided to move on.

"This just goes to show that we shall never be safe to worship in England," spoke up one of the men in the loft. "Even now some of our friends up the road are still in prison. The rest of us could be there before the night is over."

"What hurts most is seeing how our children are treated," Mrs. Brewster began. "I can stand it when neighbors turn their backs on me, but it is almost more than I can bear when the children start throwing stones at Jonathan and Patience and even at Baby Fear."

"It begins to look as if we might have to leave England," the pastor agreed. "But I am not sure where we can go. It is bad here, I know. But it is far worse in many other countries."

Slowly William Brewster, the leading citizen of Scrooby, got to his feet.

"As you all know," he began quietly, "I spent a great deal of time abroad during the five years I was at Queen Elizabeth's court. In Holland I

8

saw that men are really free to worship as they please. Many people even then were going to Holland from France and other lands."

Brewster went on to describe the beautiful cities and canals to be found in Holland and assured his friends that it would be a good place to live. There would be work for all — if not in the fishing fleets, then in the silk and woolen mills.

"Why not go to Holland?" the Scrooby Separatists began to ask each other.

2.
Escape to Holland

All summer they planned how to get out of England. It was not easy. They dared not speak openly, as King James did not like his subjects to find homes in other lands. When autumn came, crops were gathered and sold. The men secretly got rid of their horses and cattle, their furniture, and most of their other belongings. Clothing, bedding, and a few of their smaller treasures were packed into bundles that they could carry. At last they were ready to start, though they had no permission to make the journey.

They knew they had to leave England to avoid arrest, but they were sad at the thought of going. They loved their homeland. They loved the green fields and meadows around Scrooby and the homes in which they had once been happy.

"We are starting off like pilgrims now," they thought. "And like pilgrims, we must wander on and on until we find a home where we can be free to worship God as we choose."

A few nights later the stars looked down upon a strange sight. The tired wanderers had by now made their way to the seashore near the town of Boston on the east coast of England. Here they waited for the little ship which was to carry them to Holland.

Hours passed and it grew late. One by one the faint lights of the town went out and it was still and dark. Even the waves seemed to speak in whispers as they lapped against the shore.

On a wooden box sat a young mother with a sleeping baby in her arms. Two tired children with the sand for a bed and a shawl for a pillow slept beside her. Older boys and girls were too excited to sleep. Like their parents, they perched on bundles and whispered in low tones.

As the night wore on, fathers paced up and down the beach. They peered out over the black water, hoping to see the outline of the ship they had hired to take them to Holland.

A terrible fear clutched at every heart. What if the ship should never come? What if soldiers suddenly swooped down on them? Every minute they waited added to their danger.

Midnight came, then one — two — three —

and four o'clock. In the distance cocks began to crow. The men got together and began to talk in hushed voices.

"Are you sure this is the right spot?" asked Will Bradford.

"Yes, I know it is. We agreed to meet right here where this little brook flows into the sea. The captain promised he would be here without fail," whispered William Brewster.

"Well, it is almost dawn," said John Robinson, "and it begins to look as if daylight will find us still waiting on the shore."

"If the ship is not here in another hour, we must hide," warned Brewster. "Listen! I hear the splash of an oar!"

They listened, straining their ears to catch the least sound across the water. Again came the splash and their hearts were filled with hope.

A moment later a small boat approached the shore. Quickly it was loaded and rowed back to a ship that lay in deep water. Then it returned for another and still another load until all the men, women, and children with their goods had been carried out to the ship.

"Captain, hurry and get away so that we shall be safely out of the King's reach by daylight," urged Brewster.

"Don't be too sure of that!" snarled a gruff voice at his side.

In a minute the refugees were surrounded by soldiers.

"What does this mean, Captain?" cried Brewster.

But the treacherous captain was nowhere to be seen. He was so ashamed of his wicked deed that he dared not face the people whom he had betrayed into the hands of the soldiers.

The pilgrims knew they were no match for the King's men. When daylight arrived everyone was once more on shore.

When spring came, another attempt was made to leave England. This time William Brewster arranged with a Dutch captain, whom he knew, to carry them to Holland, in his ship.

Careful plans were made to meet the ship at a lonely spot on the shore between the cities of Grimsby and Hull. The women and children, with most of their possessions, traveled to the meeting place in a small boat they had hired. The men and boys planned to go overland to the meeting spot.

But again they were unlucky. The women and children arrived at the secret meeting place a day early. They had made a terrible mistake.

All that day they waited in their boat for the larger vessel, not knowing they were too early. They feared every minute that they would be taken prisoners again.

The sea was rough, and even the babies were seasick. Finally, the women begged the sailors to turn into a little creek nearby. There they were able to get over their seasickness, but found to their dismay that they were locked tight in the mud when the tide went out.

The next morning a sail appeared. The Dutch captain was coming, just as he had promised. He moved in as close to shore as he dared and waited. But the boatload of weeping women and children could not get to him. They were stuck fast until the next tide came in!

The captain swore some mighty Dutch oaths, because he knew he was taking a terrible risk in even being there. While he anxiously waited for the tide to refloat the little ship, he sent his landing boat ashore to pick up the men and boys.

One boatload of men and boys got safely aboard the Dutch vessel. The landing boat had already started back to get a second load when suddenly the Dutch captain gasped. A long black line began to curve down the hill. It was heading straight for the beach.

He could see a hundred or more horsemen. "They are coming for us!" he cried in terror.

One look told all his passengers that the King's men had again learned their secret. But they were not ready yet to give up.

"Hurry," shouted Will Bradford. "We can still get the others before the troops reach them!"

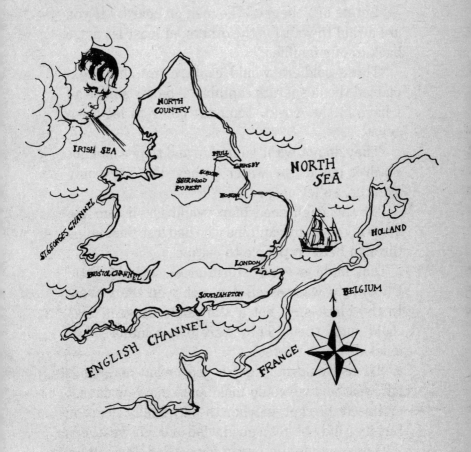

But he spoke too late. The Dutch captain had already started to lift anchor and wind filled the sails as the ship began to move.

"Let us off," begged the men on board. "If you are afraid to wait for the others, at least let us go back to our families."

"Those soldiers would capture my ship," explained the desperate captain. "And my ship is all I have in the world. I am not going to let them get it."

"They do not want your ship and they could not reach it out in the water if they did. They only want us, so let us go back!"

But the frightened man would not listen. He knew of too many captains who had lost their ships through helping people to escape.

That night a great storm arose and the little Dutch ship was tossed like a chip on the waves. In the black sky, not a star could be seen that could guide them. They were blown hundreds of miles off their course.

"If we would only get a good wind and some fair weather, we could make port in a few days," promised the captain when the sky finally cleared. But they did not get a good wind and fair weather.

That very night a heavy fog settled down upon the sea so that they could not see ten feet in front of the ship. Two days later another storm came up. It was even worse than the first one had been. Water poured in through a hole in the deck. For seven days they saw no sun, moon, or stars and sailors cried in their terror, "We sink! We sink! Lord save us!"

No one on board expected ever to see land again.

The Dutch captain thought that God was punishing him with this storm for leaving the helpless women and children to be captured by the English soldiers. He and his crew joined the men and boys in prayers for help and pardon.

At last the clouds broke and bits of blue sky could be seen. The wind died and the waves grew smaller. With the sun to guide them by day and stars by night, they finally made their way back from the coast of Norway, where they had blown, to the city of Amsterdam, in Holland.

But what had become of the women and children held fast in the muddy creek, and the men left standing on the shore? By the time the English soldiers got to the beach, they found that most of the men had slipped through their fingers. They were either on board the ship that was fast moving out to sea, or they had managed to hide somewhere on shore.

"What should I do?" the leader of the guard asked himself. "It seems wrong to put in prison women and children who have done no real harm." But he had his orders and there was nothing to do but obey.

Those captured were taken in their own little

boat, once more afloat, to the nearest town. When the soldiers looked down at their prisoners — tearful women and sick, hungry children — they did not feel very brave.

The captured ones did not stay long in jail this time. But once out, they no longer had any homes to go to in England. The judges did not know what to do with them.

"Since their husbands got away, let the women and children go to them," they ordered.

3.
A New Home

A ship, carrying the last of the Scrooby refugees, was approaching the largest city in Holland.

"If it were not for this fog, I think you could see Amsterdam by now," one of the sailors told the group of children in the bow.

They peered into the mist, but not a sign of a city could they see. Above, a ball of soft yellow light showed the spot where the sun was trying to break through the haze. Sometimes a shadowy sail floated toward them out of the mist and disappeared as quickly as it had come.

Many little fishing boats passed close by. In one sat a small boy, perched high on a pile of brown nets. He saw the children and waved.

It took a long time to reach the landing. There several English men and boys were impatiently waiting. The eyes of all children on board moved quickly from one man to the next. They were looking for a face they loved.

The Brewster children had no trouble picking out their young friend Will Bradford and waving to him. Their own father was with them, as he had stayed until the last boatload to make sure that everyone got away safely.

"I have a cottage for you," young Bradford said, as he greeted his friends. "But it is not the fine, large home that Scrooby Manor is."

"You were always a good boy, Will," the older man answered. "We do not need a large house. If the cottage will shelter you and the five of us, it is plenty large enough."

"Yes," joined in Mrs. Brewster, "we want you to make your home with us until you decide you want one of your own."

Bradford took little Fear in his arms and led the way. On many chimneys the children saw nests of sticks and straw. In some were young storks with their hungry mouths wide open for the frogs or little fishes their mothers were bringing them.

"What a queer, high road we are on!" exclaimed Patience. "I never saw a road up in the air before!"

"This road is really a dike," Will Bradford explained. "Holland is a low country; sometimes it is even lower than the sea, so people have to build these walls of earth and stone to keep the water out."

"I should think the water would push through dikes," said Jonathan.

"Sometimes it does. First there is only a tiny trickle. But if the hole is not mended at once, it grows larger and larger until there is nothing that can hold the water back."

Finally the Brewsters reached the street where they were to live. How different it seemed from the road that ran through Scrooby. Down the middle was a broad stream called a canal. On each side of the canal was a narrow path, paved with stones. There was scarcely room on the path for even a horse and cart. When people wanted to ride, or had a heavy load to carry, they had to use a boat on the canal.

The house seemed even stranger than the road. It was built on piles driven into the soft earth, and one side had settled faster than the other.

"Is our house about to fall over?" Patience whispered to her mother.

Mrs. Brewster laughed and shook her head.

When Will Bradford opened the door, they all stepped into the kitchen, which was the front room in this Dutch home. Their sitting room looked out on a tiny garden to the rear. At night the kitchen became a bedroom where queer box-like beds in the walls were opened.

At bedtime, Mrs. Brewster tucked the girls into one of the cubbyhole beds hidden in the wall behind curtains. Patience put her arms around her mother's neck and whispered, "It doesn't seem real! I'm afraid when I wake up in the morning we'll all be back in England again."

Amsterdam was home to the families from Scrooby for almost a year. Then one morning a little fleet of canal boats tied up in the streets where the English were living. The families from Scrooby were again on the move; they were going to Leyden, a beautiful city that was the new center of learning in Holland.

It did not take them long to load the boats, as they were all much poorer than they had been in England and had few belongings.

From one little canal into another they sailed until Amsterdam was left far behind. Then they passed into a broad canal that looked like a ribbon stretched across the green meadows. In every direction were windmills. Sometimes they stood alone; sometimes they stood in groups, looking for all the world like a family of giants against the sky!

As the barges came nearer to the city of Leyden, those on board saw a strange sight. Close beside a large garden bright with flowers was a field which seemed to be covered with snow. They knew it was not flowers. What could it be?

As the barges drew nearer, the passengers saw long pieces of white linen bleaching in the sun.

The white meadow was cloth that had been woven in the mills of Leyden.

Leyden was a beautiful city with a great university, but it proved a harder place than Amsterdam in which to earn a living. William Brewster, who had a good education, taught English and printed books. But most of the men who had been simple farmers in England found that they had to go to work in the mills. There were not many jobs open to them because they were not citizens of Holland.

Some got jobs washing wool, as it was very dirty when clipped from the sheep. Others combed it. Still others spun it into thread, while many of the men wove the thread into cloth. Will Bradford, by now a young man of nearly twenty, got a job making "fustian," a kind of corduroy.

Work started as soon as it was light in the morning and continued until dark. And still the families found that they were able to earn so little money that even the boys and girls had to go to work in the mills. Children became bent and old long before their time and lost the ruddy cheeks they had had in England.

The Scrooby congregation in Leyden bought a large house on Bell Alley. It was called *Groenepoort*, or Green Gate, and stood in the old part of the city opposite the cathedral, *Pieterskerk*. Behind its garden was an empty lot into which they crowded many dollsize houses, one almost on top of the next. The poorest members of the group lived in these houses. From the upper windows of the *Pieterskerk*, Green Gate looked like an old mother hen with more than a dozen chickens!

Green Gate was both house and church. The pastor, John Robinson, and his family lived upstairs; the large rooms on the first floor were used for worship.

Life was hard in Holland, but the Dutch people were kind to them. And here, at last, they could worship God as they pleased.

4.
Goodbye to Holland

At first, everything in Holland had seemed strange to the Pilgrims — gaily colored houses with their floors of tile and their steep roofs, the dikes and canals and giant windmills. And everywhere the clatter of wooden shoes. But strangest of all was the new language.

Goede morgen, Good morning.

Danke U wel, Thank you very much.

Goede dag, Goodbye.

Over and over they would repeat the words and wonder if they would ever be able to talk with their Dutch neighbors. The children learned quickly, and after they had lived in Holland a few years the language and customs no longer seemed strange. They were becoming Hollanders!

English children grew to like the Dutch dress and the big wooden shoes. They liked Dutch food and winter skating on canals and the funny little Dutch wallbeds.

Even Jonathan and Patience were beginning to forget Scrooby. The coach from London, the waiting at the gate for the King's messenger, Robin Hood and Sherwood Forest — all this seemed like something they had dreamed. Little Fear Brewster and her two baby brothers — Love and Wrestling — scarcely knew that they were not Hollanders.

More years went by and many of the boys and girls who had fled England with their parents in 1607 and 1608 had grown up and married. Will Bradford and Jonathan Brewster had their own families. Their babies would learn to speak Dutch better than English.

The older people were heartbroken. They wanted their families to remain English and to keep their old English customs and language. Many of them did not feel as well and strong as they had before they started working the long hours in the Dutch mills. They longed to get back on farms so they could work out of doors again, as they had done in England. But they were too poor to buy farms in Holland.

Sometimes they would talk about the New World on the other side of the Atlantic. They had heard of the daring adventures of Sir Walter Raleigh and knew men were already making settlements in Virginia, Florida, the Caribbean Islands, and South America.

"If we could get to America, perhaps we could have homes like the ones we had in England," they thought. "We could have our own church, and it would be easier to bring up our children to love and serve God."

But could they bear to go so far away? The New World was thousands of miles from both Holland and England. They thought of the dear friends and neighbors whom they would have to leave behind and never see again. They thought of the terrible hardships that they would have to face on an ocean voyage. They thought of the Indians living in the New World. These Indians were savage and cruel, they had been told. They even ate people alive, or so the books said.

"Perhaps if we treated them like brothers, they would be our friends," suggested John Robinson. "Indians are human, the same as you and I."

For several years the people at the Green Gate in Leyden talked about going to America. At first it was only a dream. Poor as they were, they did not see how they could ever get a ship in which to cross the ocean. But other groups seemed able to do it. So some of the leaders from the Green Gate crossed to England to see what they could arrange. They found that it was very hard to get permission from the government to start a colony, and even harder to get money to outfit an expedition.

Businessmen were afraid to lend money because many earlier colonizers had taken sick and died far from home. Most of the survivors had given up and returned to England.

"Do not worry about us," William Brewster wrote at this time to important people in England. "We are not like the others. We have courage enough to face whatever may happen. We shall not return!"

Finally, a man named Thomas Weston said he would put up the money needed. Weston was a wealthy London hardware merchant who had money to invest. He set hard terms. He agreed that he and his partners would advance much of the money needed if the settlers, in turn, would promise to work for them for seven years — fishing, lumbering, farming, fur trading, or anything else they could find to do.

Nothing the settlers made or earned all these seven long years would be their own. Even the clothes on their backs and the food they ate and the houses they built with their own hands would belong to the common fund. At the end of seven years, Weston said, they would settle their accounts and the colonists who had worked under this scheme would each receive a very small share. Everything else would belong to him and the other London investors.

This was almost the same as slavery and the people knew it.

"At least let us keep our homes and gardens as our very own," they begged.

"No," said Weston. "These are our terms and you can accept them or leave them." He knew how to drive a hard bargain and he would not budge.

Weston's harsh terms made many people change their minds about going. At first everyone had liked the idea. Now only a few of those who had wanted to go to the New World would sell seven years of their lives to cross the ocean.

William Brewster, who had written so bravely to a friend, "We have courage enough to face whatever may happen," was one of the first to say that he and his family would accept Weston's terms and would go. So did the Bradfords, the Carvers, the Cushmans, the Allertons, and the Winslows. But many at Green Gate in Leyden decided that they preferred to stay in Holland, at least for the time being.

The beloved pastor, John Robinson, had intended to go but when he found that most of the members of his congregation were staying in Holland, he changed his mind. He and his family would stay on at the Green Gate and would come over later if all went well.

William Brewster was an elder in the church. Until John Robinson joined the colony or they got another pastor, he would be able to lead their worship.

When Weston and his partners heard that so few were going, they said there were not enough to form a colony. For a while it looked as if the plans would have to be dropped. Then Weston decided to advertise in London. He opened the colony to anyone who would agree to his terms. They did not have to be Separatists and worship as the others did.

This was sad news to the little group at the

Green Gate in Leyden who had made the first plans. They dreaded having to take dozens of strangers with them, people whom they had never seen or heard of before. These people might have very different beliefs and perhaps different customs.

Again they had to decide. Which did they want more: to be by themselves or to get to the New World? Weston gave them no choice. Unless the Strangers, as they started to call them, went along, the whole trip would be canceled.

They decided to accept the Strangers. After all, these people might not be so bad, they told each other. In fact, it was possible that some of them might be very nice people! If any really bad ones came along, they would have to handle that problem when it came up.

Once having decided to go, they spent months in planning and preparation. It proved a harder job to outfit a colony than any of them had expected. And now they had two groups making plans, one in England and one in Holland.

Those at Green Gate decided to buy a sturdy little boat that would take them to England to join the main party. There they would divide, some getting on a larger ship that the group in England would only charter instead of buying outright.

The plan was for the two vessels to form a kind of convoy for the dangerous journey across the Atlantic. The larger, hired ship would then return to England. The smaller vessel could be used for fishing up and down the Atlantic coast.

Working under this plan, the Leyden group bought the *Speedwell*, which was small and rotted and in generally poor condition. They had it beached and overhauled. After scrubbing and patching and calking were finished, tall, extra-heavy masts and new sails were added.

Meanwhile in England the *Mayflower* was being chartered. She was a freighter of 180 tons which had been used to carry wine for many years. The captain was Christopher Jones, part-owner as well as captain. He was a good captain and a kind and generous man. If it had not been for him, the Pilgrims would probably all have died during the first winter!

In the seventeenth century there were no stores where food for a ship could be bought. Wheat had to be bought from farmers and ground and baked into a kind of bread called "hardtack." Butter had to be bought and packed. Cattle had to be bought on the hoof, and then a butcher had to be found to slaughter them and salt or pickle the meat and pack it into barrels that they could carry. This meat was called "salt horse" by the sailors.

Food had to be carried, not only for the trip across the ocean, but for all of the first year in America, as they would arrive too late to plant a crop in 1620. A steady diet of hardtack, butter, and "salt horse" day after day would not be good. But it was the best they could do. A few of the families were able to add a few private luxuries such as dried fruits, sugar, and lemons.

Water was a problem. Water, they were told, soon became stagnant on long sea voyages; so they carried beer as well. Beer was the common drink of the day, as neither tea nor coffee had yet been introduced into England.

To look after the hundreds of barrels and casks in which the food and drink were packed on the *Mayflower*, a "cooper," or barrel maker, had to be hired. They found a powerful, blond young man who said he would like a chance to see the New World. His name was John Alden.

Then, to take charge of any military defense that might be required in the new colony, a professional soldier was hired. The short, redheaded, fearless man was Myles Standish.

While leaders were busy buying provisions in England, every family worked frantically to get together the things it would need. They worked as people would today if they had to pack in a few bundles and boxes everything they would take to another planet.

Hundreds of items were checked off: kettles, skillets, bellows, tongs, bottles, cups, trenchers, tubs. Then there must be bedding and linen. There must be all the special things needed for babies and toddlers.

While the women were adding item after item to their lists, their husbands were busy, too. They would need saws, axes, hammers, hatchets, grindstones, anvils, and perhaps even a giant screw if they were to put up houses and sheds. They would need lines and hooks for fishing, and of course each man would have to provide the best he could in the way of armor and weapons.

Everybody would need clothes. Mothers worked day and night trying to finish enough garments to last their families at least a year.

"Our clothes must be warm and sturdy," they reminded each other, "because we will have no time to sew when we get there."

They chose dark colors — deep rich reds, wines, russets, browns, greens, and black — so that dirt would not show much.

The *Speedwell* was finally loaded in July and ready to sail. Within a few days, if their luck held, the group from Leyden would join the group from England at Southampton, England, where the *Mayflower* would be waiting.

This was a sad day at the Green Gate. Many families and friends were being separated, perhaps never to see each other again. Jonathan Brewster and his teen-age sisters, Patience and Fear, were staying in Holland. If all went well, they hoped to join their parents and brothers in a year or two.

The Bradford family, too, was being broken.

Dorothy and Will Bradford had talked day after day and had finally agreed that it would be best to leave their little boy with friends in Leyden. But when the moment of parting came, Mrs. Bradford was not sure they had made the right decision. He was so small and frail and dear to their hearts! The mother would never forget how she felt when the child was pulled from her arms as the ship was about to sail. At night she would dream of him and see before her the pitiful look on the little face when he realized his mother and father were leaving without him.

As the *Speedwell* pulled away from Delft Haven, the port twenty miles from Leyden, where the ship had been loading, even the sternest of the men were weeping.

Less than fifty men, women, and children were on their way. They watched the figures on shore grow smaller and smaller until they could see them no more.

5.
Voyage
of the *Mayflower*

When the *Speedwell* reached Southampton, the *Mayflower* was already there waiting. Some of the Leyden Pilgrims moved into the larger, less crowded ship. Meanwhile the leaders were trying to get their debts paid so that the ships would be free to sail. The passengers looked each other over and started to get acquainted.

Nine or ten families and a number of single men had been added to the expedition in England. Some of these people were already known to those on board the *Speedwell*. Others were total strangers, the ones Weston had recruited in London and southern England.

A few of the Weston recruits, like the Billingtons and their two boys, caused nothing but trouble. But there were many fine families among the Strangers.

Now there were more children on board, too.

There were three in the Hopkins family when they started the voyage: Constance, Giles, and Damaris. The Chiltons had a lively fifteen-year-old, Mary. The Mullins family added two more: Joseph, a six-year-old, and Priscilla, who was almost eighteen.

Hardly had the two ships started when the *Speedwell* began to leak. Nobody could find a hole in it, but water continued to rise slowly until it crept around the boxes and bundles.

"I shall have to turn back," the captain stated, "so that we can repair the damage."

The leaks were mended and the two ships set sail for America a second time. They had gone about three hundred miles, and again had to turn back. Men pumped water from the *Speedwell* as fast as they could, but it gained on them.

"There is nothing to do but turn back or we shall all drown," warned the captain again.

The captain of the *Mayflower* did not want to leave the stricken ship, so both vessels returned to England. Shipbuilders were called to go over the *Speedwell*.

"It carries too heavy a mast for so small a ship," said one.

"It also has too much sail," said another.

"Maybe the trouble is partly with the hull," said a third. "But whatever is wrong, it will take several months to get it into good enough shape for crossing the ocean."

What could the poor Pilgrims do? The fine summer weather was fast slipping away. Even if they got started that very moment, they would not reach the New World before the winter storms set in. They did not dare wait if they were going to go at all.

The *Mayflower* could not carry all the passengers from both ships, and there was no money to charter another one. A few families said they would gladly wait until a later time. They were already so frightened that they welcomed any excuse to stay behind.

A few more who were weak or sickly, or who had many small children, were asked to drop out. It seemed best to the leaders to leave behind the ones least fitted to survive the dangers that lay ahead. All the rest of the men, women, and children, with their boxes, bundles, and pets, were crowded into the *Mayflower*, which set sail for the third time. Now she carried 102 passengers.

This time there was no turning back.

Pilgrims were everywhere! On this tiny freighter there were only a few passenger bunks in one cabin. Most of the women with small children were jammed into this cabin. All the rest "camped out" as best they could. Some slept between decks and some of the boys and younger men curled up in the bottom of the *shallop*, a fishing boat which had been stowed on the gun deck.

The *Mayflower* was well armed. She carried large guns called "minions," which would shoot cannon balls at any attacking pirate ship. She also had smaller guns called "sakers," as well as a supply of muskets and cutlasses to use in hand-to-hand combat.

For the first week or two there was good weather and the *Mayflower*'s sails carried the ship across the water like a great sea bird. Then a storm hit and the sky grew black, as the fierce westerly gales swept down upon the *Mayflower*.

John Howland, one of the laborers, brought along to do the heavy work for the Carver family, decided he could not stay below deck any longer. The ship had been rolling from side to side for many days, and seasick men, women, and children were sprawled everywhere.

As he crawled on deck he thought how wild and terrible the storm was. One minute the *Mayflower* was riding high on the crest of a wave. The next, with a sickening smack that made his teeth chatter, the ship dropped into the valley between two waves. Howland looked around him and leaped as he saw one wave, greater than any of the others, about to break over the ship. He tried desperately to reach safety but it was too late. With a crash like thunder the wave struck the ship and swept him overboard.

"Help, help!" he frantically screamed. "Help!"

If only someone would hear his voice above the

roar of the storm! As he toppled over the side, he grabbed the rope tied to one of the sails and hung on. But it was no use. The water closed over his head and down he went, deeper and deeper into the sea. His lungs were bursting. His strength was going fast. Had no one heard him? Would no one come to his rescue? Would they miss him tomorrow and start hunting and never know what had happened to him?

Just then he felt a tug on the rope. "Hold on, Howland, hold on," two seamen were bellowing as they pulled on the line.

Howland did hold on, though his hands were stiff with cold and the waves beat him back from the ship. One strong seaman risked his own life leaning far out to grab him. Strong arms had hold of him. At last he lay on the deck, half-frozen but still alive.

On and on the ship sailed. Some days were full of sunshine and the sea was smooth. Then mothers were able to cook, building little fires in sandboxes below deck. How good hot stew tasted after days of gnawing on cheese and hardtack!

The children begged to play outside after weeks below deck, but the crew said no. It was bad enough, they thought, having 102 people jammed in where there was space for a dozen at most. They weren't going to put up with more than thirty young ones running around getting in the way.

Sometimes Priscilla Mullins would keep them quiet by telling stories about what she did when she was a little girl. Even the tired mothers who were too far away to hear the words of the story would smile as they looked at Priscilla's laughing eyes.

"What a comfort that Mullins girl is," they said to each other.

Then Mary Chilton would take her turn and John Alden, the cooper, would whittle out a puzzle or a toy from some of his barrel staves. Even some of the sailors who had said they hated the children and wished they were all dead relented enough to teach the boys how to tie knots.

And so the long weeks dragged by. There was no heat on the *Mayflower*, no toilet except a bucket that had to be emptied overboard, no bathroom, no way to get cleaned up. Like their parents, the children wore the same clothes day after day, week after week, getting dirtier and shabbier all the time.

All night, every night, someone was coughing, as nearly everyone had caught cold. When tired children cried in their sleep, "I want to go home, Mama," weary mothers tried to soothe them so they would not wake all the others.

One day, when the voyage was nearly over, there was a big surprise. The Hopkinses had a baby brother! Giles wanted to name him "Dick," after his cat back home. But that name did not please his parents at all. Some of the children who had been born in Holland suggested "Jan." But Elizabeth and Stephen Hopkins liked that even less than they liked "Dick."

"This is an English baby and not a Dutch baby," they said.

Then someone suggested, "Why not give him a new name, one that nobody has ever had before?" What could it be? *"Mayflower?"* No, that sounded too much like a girl's name.

"This will never do," thought Mrs. Hopkins when another week passed and still the baby had no name. "Constance, you have never told us what you would like to call your baby brother."

"Oh, I think Ocean would be as good a name as any!"

"Ocean?" Mrs. Hopkins laughed. "What a queer-sounding name that is. I am sure no other child in the world has ever been called Ocean."

When Elder Brewster heard of the new suggestion he was pleased. "Maybe I can help you," he said. "I know of a word in another language that means ocean. It would make a better sounding name. It is Oceanus."

"Oceanus Hopkins! That is a good name!" exclaimed the baby's father. And so for the short year that he lived, the first Pilgrim boy was called Oceanus.

Not many days later another baby was born on the *Mayflower*, which was by that time at anchor off Cape Cod. He also had to have a name.

"Wandering, let's call him Wandering!" suggested several of the children at once. "Wandering, because that's what we are always doing!"

Mrs. White did not like Wandering for a name and so for the second time the oldest Pilgrim on the ship was asked for his advice. Did he know another nice-sounding word that meant the same as Wandering?

This time Mr. Brewster suggested Peregrine.

"Peregrine White and Oceanus Hopkins! What big names for such tiny red babies," thought most of the children.

6.
First Days
in the New World

On the morning of November twenty-first, anxious-faced Pilgrims lined the rails. In a few hours they would set foot in the New World — after three years of working and planning and dreaming. Already the *Mayflower* had rounded the tip of Cape Cod and would soon drop anchor in Cape Cod harbor.

Tired mothers wiped their eyes while children shouted and squealed in excitement. Giles and Will and the Billington boys became so excited trying to "help" that Captain Jones bellowed for everybody underfoot to get back — or get below.

The Pilgrim leaders were worried. Ever since Captain Jones had swung the *Mayflower* around when it was heading into the shoals off the "elbow" of the Cape, a few of the Strangers had been plotting. The leaders did not know how many were in the plot, but they did know trouble was coming.

At first there were only whispers. Then the whispers grew louder and more defiant. Two of the men began to boast.

"Just wait," one threatened. "As soon as I set foot on land, I'm off. I'll do what I please, and none of these long-faced holy Saints, as they call themselves, will give me orders! I'll show a few of 'em around here who is boss!"

The speaker was seconded by one of his friends. "He's right. Is this Virginia? No! Our papers say we are to go to Virginia, remember? But if we ain't in Virginia, we don't have to go by those papers."

Another one asked, "Is that true? You mean our papers aren't good outside Virginia?" Turning to a fourth he began, "Did you hear, they can't hold us. This is New England!"

"Virginia or New England, there is not going to be any mutiny on board the *Mayflower*," growled John Carver as he, Bradford, Brewster, and a few others held a hasty conference.

"We are here to form a colony and together we must stay," they agreed. But they knew they had no permission to settle in New England. They would have to act fast.

First they borrowed Captain Jones's cabin so they could work away from the others. Then after a few minutes William Brewster slipped below and brought up his writing materials.

The plotters could hear voices rising and falling.

45

They could hear the scratch of the quill pen. But try as hard as they could, they could not make out what was taking place in the secret meeting.

Ten minutes became twenty, then thirty, then forty. The Strangers, who had been boasting an hour before, were becoming uneasy. What was going on in the captain's quarters? Things were not turning out at all as they had planned.

Finally, an order was given for all men to assemble; not women and children and babies — just men.

They filed into the captain's cabin. Those who could not squeeze in crowded around the door. What was said in that cabin during the next hour will never be known. To this day it has remained a carefully guarded Pilgrim secret!

But when the Pilgrims — Saints and Strangers — filed out of the captain's cabin, even the worst trouble-makers had signed an agreement among themselves to work together for the common good and to obey the officers whom they would elect. John Carver was the one they had chosen to be governor of the colony for the first year.

Now the Pilgrims were ready to go ashore. A boat was lowered and a landing party of fifteen or sixteen crawled aboard. As soon as their feet touched land, they fell to their knees.

"O God, our Heavenly Father," they prayed as

they knelt on the beach, "we bless Thee for having brought us over the vast and furious ocean safely to this New World."

The landing party saw whales and many birds. They sampled the mussels they found, which made them sick. They gathered great armloads of sweet-smelling juniper and took it back for firewood. But they did not see a living person.

The next day was Sunday.

Monday morning the sun was warm and bright and the children begged to be taken ashore to run and play. Mothers also looked longingly toward land, as they had seen a good place to do their washing. Not a bit of washing had been done on the *Mayflower* for over two months!

In no time at all piles of dirty clothes had been gathered, and tubs, pails, and soap were loaded into the boat and rowed ashore. Soon fires were snapping and crackling under kettles of water as children heaped driftwood on them. Water began to bubble. All morning the scrubbing, boiling, and rinsing continued until every tub was empty and the last dirty little garment had been wrung and spread to dry.

While the women washed the clothing and the children ran up and down the beach under the watchful eyes of two men who stood guard, Myles Standish and a party of sixteen went exploring.

They had followed the curve of the beach for

about a mile when Bradford's sharp eyes suddenly spotted something moving ahead of them. One, two, three, four, five INDIANS!

"Perhaps this means work for my trusty sword," said Myles Standish, as he reached for his weapon.

"Put it away, Standish," said Bradford quietly. "We need to make friends with these people if we can. Maybe we will be able to buy some food from them."

The Pilgrims wanted to meet the Indians, for they were the first people they had seen since they landed. But the Indians did not want to meet the Pilgrims. The Indians whistled to their dog, which had dashed ahead to greet the Pilgrims' spaniel, and Indians and dog slipped noiselessly into the thicket. The men from the *Mayflower* did their best to follow, but the weight of their armor made them no match for the nimble, sure-footed Indians.

That night the scouting party camped in the open but were careful to keep two guards on duty all the time.

The next morning they marched on, heading farther south. They passed fields where corn had recently been grown, but they did not see an Indian or a house of any kind.

They did not see the Indians, but black eyes were peering out of bushes and from behind trees all along their line of march. Through bogs and bushes and up and down hills they dragged, their armor becoming more scratched and snagged the farther they went.

At one point they came to a field where a house had once stood; there were still four or five rotted old planks laid together. Here they also found a large kettle like the ones used to feed the crew on ships.

One man, scouting a little ahead of the others, found a heap of sand that showed marks of hands where it had been smoothed.

"Maybe you've found an Indian grave," someone suggested.

"No, the mound can't be a grave; it is much too short and round. Do you suppose it would be all right to open it and see what is hidden below?"

They hacked away at the frozen ground, and were disappointed at first to find only a worn little basket of Indian corn.

But Stephen Hopkins continued to dig, and below the first basket was still another one, large and new and full of fine new ears of corn — some yellow, some red, and some mixed with blue. The basket was shaped like a bottle, round and narrow at the top. It held three or four bushels of this odd-looking corn, or "maize," as the Pilgrims called it.

They had heard about it but had never seen it before. They tried a few kernels between their teeth and found it dry and hard to chew. But after having lived since summer on hardtack and "salt horse," even dried corn tasted very good.

"God has been good," they thought again, for they were running low on food on the *Mayflower*. But would it be right to help themselves to the corn? Maybe this corn was something the Indians themselves needed to keep from starving.

After much argument among themselves they decided that it would be all right to take part of the corn if they came back and paid for it when they discovered the rightful owners. So they filled the kettle, and two men carried it on a pole.

For a second night the scouting party had to sleep on the trail and again they took turns keeping watch so there would be no surprise attack. It began to rain and the men were soaked to the skin; they huddled as close to the fire as they dared.

The next morning, still stiff with cold, they plodded back toward the ship. As they wandered across the meadows and through the thickets, they came to one queer-looking tree where a young shoot had been strangely bent down and some acorns strewn beneath it.

"What do you suppose this means?" Bradford asked as he stepped forward to examine it.

Snap! Crash! Suddenly Bradford was dangling high in the air, his head nearly touching the ground. He had stumbled on an Indian deer trap that sprang when his foot touched it.

"Help! Help! Get me down from here," he yelled frantically.

His friend Myles Standish wanted to laugh at this strange "deer" thrashing about in the air, and probably would have if the accident had not been so serious. Instead, he dashed forward and, slashing away with his sword, soon had a red-faced and puffing Bradford right-side-up again.

7.
Narrow Escape

Ten days went by. Days were growing very short and it was dark and dreary. Much of the time it rained. Some days the rain turned to fog, some days to sleet. Soon there would be a blanket of deep snow over trails and fallen leaves.

"You will have to hurry and find a place to settle, as it is now well into December," warned Captain Jones. "It will not be safe much longer for us to anchor here."

On the morning of December eighth a party of thirty-four men, including Captain Jones and some of the *Mayflower* crew, began another long expedition. On the third day out they reached "Cornhill," as they called the spot where the first group had found the kettle and the Indian corn.

This time they dug up still more corn, getting about ten bushels in all, as well as a bag of beans and a bottle of oil. Again they felt guilty at robbing the Indians. Again they agreed that if they did take the food, they would have to make payment for it later.

Many of the men found they could not continue the trip. They were suffering from scurvy and exhaustion and colds and a few even had pneumonia. So Captain Jones took back to the *Mayflower* fifteen of those who could not go on.

Eighteen who were still reasonably well and strong continued the march.

They found two graves that puzzled them. In one was a man and in the other a child, but they were both light-haired! The Pilgrims knew there were no blond Indians. Who could they be? Were they fellow-English off some fishing vessel that had been wrecked or had put in here for supplies? Had they taken ill and died and then been carefully buried? Or had they been murdered? Whoever they were, they had not been dumped in a hole with sod thrown over them. They had received a very careful Indian burial. Here was a mystery that made the Pilgrims shiver, and which they never were able to solve.

A little farther along, they found two deserted Indian homes. They were not tepees, such as the Indians on the Western Plains built. These were huts, made from sapling trees. The framework had been carefully covered from the ground to the rounded top with thick, carefully made mats. The doors also were mats that would swing open and shut.

The chimneys on these Indian houses were simply wide-open holes at the top of the huts, with a mat that could be placed over the opening, like a cover to a box, when no fire was burning. The huts were high enough for a man to stand upright in them and move about.

In the middle of the room were four little stakes which had been pounded into the ground. Sticks were laid across them on which cooking pots were hung. Round about the fire on the ground, the Indians had scattered mats. The Pilgrims guessed these had been used as beds.

These Indian houses had double walls. There was a layer of thin mats on the inside, and a rough outside covering made of great slabs of tree bark.

In the houses the Pilgrims found wooden bowls, trays, and earthen pots, baskets made of crab shells worked together, large storage baskets, several deer head and feet, and the claws of an eagle and other "ornaments." Searching further, the Pilgrims came across two or three baskets of parched acorns, some pieces of fish, and some broiled herring, which showed that this was not a deserted camp. Indians had been sleeping and eating here not long before. In one hut was a pile of sedges and other materials for making mats. There were also several different kinds of seed.

One they recognized as tobacco seed; some of the others were strange to them.

"I cannot understand it. I cannot make out what has happened," Bradford repeated over and over as he prowled about the Indian dwellings. "People live here. We have found their homes and their graves and their food! But where are they? Where has every living person disappeared to?"

While some of the men were making these discoveries and others were busy putting their equipment into shape after the rough voyage across the Atlantic, the children on the *Mayflower* found it hard to stay cooped up in the ship.

Francis Billington seemed to get into more trouble than any of the others. If he started to cut his name on the ship, someone was sure to call out, "Stop it!" If he darted out on deck and began to climb a mast, a sailor would grab him by the scruff of the neck and with a mighty oath shove him below again. Even when he just wanted to get a good look at the brand-new baby Peregrine, and started to pick it up by an ear, the baby's mother gave a blood-curdling scream and slapped his hands!

"No, no, no! Stop it, Francis! Get down, Francis. Be quiet, Francis. Get away, Francis! That is all I hear all day long," he said to himself as he sneaked down where the guns were kept.

In his hands he held some wild-duck feathers.

He thought it would be great fun to fill the quills with gunpowder and make firecrackers. He called them "squibs."

This time there was nobody around to shout, "Stop it, Francis!"

He soon found an open keg of gunpowder and began to fill his squibs. It was hard to make the powder go into the little quills; most of it spilled on the floor instead.

When the squibs were filled, Francis noticed several old muskets hanging on a wall. "How those girls and women will jump if I shoot off one of these guns," he thought.

It was hard to shoot a musket, particularly hard for a small boy. But this did not stop Francis. He knew where to find a slow-burning fuse, and away he darted to get it. Soon he was back, carrying the lighted fuse right into the powder room.

He never stopped to think. If he had, he would have known that one little spark in the gunpowder would have blown the whole ship, and everyone in it, into a million pieces.

Francis climbed up on some boxes and took down an old musket. It was loaded, for Captain Myles Standish had it ready in case of sudden danger. Francis knew he could fire it; hadn't he seen the men fire muskets many times?

"I'll make this old musket talk," he whispered to himself.

Then came a blinding flash and boom! Bang!

Snap! Crack! Bang! When the thick smoke had cleared a little, an angry sailor found a very frightened boy lying on the deck. Francis did not know how he came to be lying there in a heap. He knew only that his eyes were smarting and his hands and shoulder were sore.

Mothers with white faces and trembling hands ran to quiet screaming children. The crew darted from deck to deck hunting for leaks in the ship.

But wonder of wonders, no great harm had been done. The squibs were gone, the musket had gone off, the powder on the floor had flashed up and burned out — but they had not set fire to the deadly powder keg.

"If that keg had exploded, we would not have to worry about where we are going to settle," barked Myles Standish when he looked over the damage. "It is lucky that we are still alive."

"It is the mercy of God," said Elder Brewster.

8.
Landing at Plymouth

I t was now the middle of December and growing
colder all the time. It began to snow and great
white flakes covered the ground with a blanket.
But still the Pilgrims had not found a place to build
their homes that would meet all their needs.

"We must have woods nearby so that we can
cut lumber for building our village, and also have
logs to burn for firewood," said Elder Brewster.

"But the forest should not be too near, because
we need land for crops," reminded Bradford. "And
we must have a safe harbor for our boats, as well
as a good stream of fresh water."

"Most important of all is a hill," spoke up Myles
Standish. "On a hill we can build a fort. And a
fort will be necessary to protect us from attacks
from either land or sea."

No matter which way the men turned, they did
not seem to find the right spot. Finally, they de-

cided to send out still another exploring party. Eighteen men set off in the shallop. They got soaked to the skin getting into the boat and then their clothing froze to them as stiff as boards.

The first night they threw up a rough stockade and kept guards posted all the time they slept, because they thought they had seen ten or twelve Indians from a distance.

As the guards walked up and down, the light from the campfire fell on the tired faces of the men curled in a circle around the fire. The flickering light touched the distant tree trunks and stretched long black shadows across the frozen ground.

The guards saw shining eyes peering at them from the darkness. "Wolves? Lions? Tigers? Or just foxes?" they asked each other, for they did not know what strange animals might be lurking in this new land. It was wolves' eyes they saw, but the animals kept their distance.

Several times during the night the guards thought they heard Indians. But no one attacked.

Finally morning came. With daylight the wolves slunk away. The exhausted Pilgrims, stiff with cold, went on with their search for a good building site.

Another day passed — and still they had not found the right place.

That night they were not far from the spot where they had slept the night before. They again put up a fence of sticks and twigs around their campfire and set guards to watch all night. There were many sounds that night. Within the camp there was coughing — the hacking coughs of men whose wet clothing had frozen to their backs two days before. At a distance there was the yelping and whining of wild animals. And once the guards jumped to alert because they thought they heard Indians sneaking up for attack.

While it was still dark, they broke camp. Some of the men, thinking that it would help them to get off to an early start, dragged their armor and equipment down to the beach and then came back to the camp for breakfast.

Nobody, not even Myles Standish, thought the Indians would choose that moment to attack, as long as they had not bothered them during the night. Just then one of the stragglers yelled, "Indians! Indians!"

Those who had taken their armor and weapons down to the boat ran wildly to get them. Careful Myles Standish and a few others who had taken no chances hurriedly buckled on their armor and seized their guns. Men were dashing about every which way, bumping into each other.

Nobody thought about breakfast or even about how cold he was.

From tree to tree, the Indians slipped nearer. As they advanced, they yelled something that sounded to the Pilgrims like, "Woach! Woach ha! ha! Hach! Woach!"

Nobody knew what it meant. But they all guessed it meant something like, "Death, death! We've got you this time. And we shall kill all of you!"

Indian arrows were flying in all directions.

Pilgrim muskets were returning the fire. In the faint morning light the Pilgrims saw thirty or forty savages moving from tree to tree.

"Ping!" sounded their arrows as they flew thick and fast. One struck Myles Standish above the heart, but thanks to his armor it did no harm.

One Pilgrim hit the tree that the Indian leader was hiding behind. The bark splintered and the Indian gave a horrible scream of pain — or rage. At their leader's cry, the Indians turned and fled as quickly as they had come. A few of the Pilgrims gave chase but never caught up.

"Armor was never meant to run in," puffed Edward Winslow as he and Bradford plodded back to camp.

Before starting out, the men picked up eighteen arrows — a nice souvenir that they sent back to England when the *Mayflower* sailed for home. Those who had not managed to get their coats before the attack found them hanging where they had left them — pierced with arrows. But not one Pilgrim had been injured. By the time the sun was up, the scouting party was again on its way. They packed their gear in the shallop and now headed west along the inner curve of Cape Cod.

It began to snow and a terrible storm made the waves rise higher and higher. One struck the shallop with such force that the rudder broke. Tossing helplessly, the men tried to steer with oars. The storm grew worse and the mast snapped off, toppling with the sail into the water. The crest of each wave lifted the helpless boat high into the air; then with a mighty slap it dropped into the trough. Some of the men clutched the sides of the boat and waited for the crash that would be the end.

It was almost a miracle that the shallop did not overturn or get dashed to pieces on the rocks. The stronger men pulled on the oars with all their strength and worked the shallop toward the place that is now called Clark's Island.

Their danger was not over. It was growing dark and they did not see that they were being swept toward breakers crashing over a hidden sandbar. If these breakers caught a boat, it would have no chance. Even a boat as large as a shallop would be torn to bits, and every man on board would be drowned in the icy waters of the bay.

Nearer and nearer they came to death. Then one sailor — nobody recorded his name — shouted over the roar of the storm, "About with her!"

Some of the rowers heard him. And every man who held an oar pulled with every bit of strength he had. Slowly, slowly, the shallop turned and slipped from the path of the breakers into the calm water in the lee of the island.

Drenched, half-frozen, the Pilgrim leaders and the sailors from the *Mayflower* who had come with them on this trip crawled up the beach. Many of them were too weak to stand.

A few had the strength to gather wood, and a fire was started in a sheltered spot in the snow. This helped a little to dry them out.

Some men were so ill that their friends had to drag them close to the fire. There was nothing else they could do to help them.

The next day the sun came out and it turned warm again. The Pilgrims gave thanks to God for guiding them through the terrible night, repeating together:

O give thanks unto the Lord, for he is good: for his mercy endureth for ever. (Psalm 107)

Those who were well enough began to look around.

They were on an island. In the dark of the storm they had believed this to be part of the mainland. Instead, they found they had taken shelter on a good-sized island where there were many Indian fields. But no Indians.

Monday morning, December twenty-first, the bay was blue and sparkling, though still rough. The exploring party managed, on this day, to reach the mainland, but everybody was so busy no one thought to note the exact spot.

They found deserted fields and pasture, a brook of clear water, and a hill or two. After drinking from the brook, the Pilgrims went to the top of the hill. They could see up and down the shore for many miles. There were broad meadows, more brooks to the north and to the south, great patches of woods, and what seemed to be a safe harbor for boats.

There were many signs of Indians — wild plum and cherry trees, the remains of neglected gardens, and stubble in some of the fields. There were even some human bones scattered about. But there were no people to be seen anywhere.

"There is some strange mystery here," said Governor Carver, shaking his head. "This has been an Indian town, and for a long time, too, or I miss my guess. But where has everybody gone? A whole village does not just disappear into thin air — not unless it is wiped out by an enemy or some deadly sickness."

9.
Christmas
on the *Mayflower*

In spite of the storm that had nearly cost their lives, the men were happy. At last they had found a place to settle. They could hardly wait to get back on board the *Mayflower* to tell the good news. How happy everyone would be to leave the ship! They all needed room to stretch, and clean air to breathe.

"Why, every time I stretch an arm, I bang somebody on the nose," thought young Ned Dotey, one of Mr. Hopkins's servants. "You can bet I'd never have come — they couldn't even have dragged me — if I had known it would be like this. Three months it is already that we've been jammed between decks with nearly thirty yapping, sniffling young 'uns!"

While Ned Dotey was feeling sorry for himself, Governor Carver was talking. "If I am not mistaken," he was saying, "this bay already has a

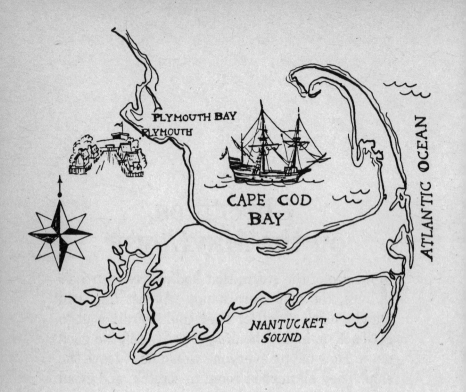

name. Captain John Smith called it Plymouth Bay on his charts after stopping here a few years back."

Most of the Pilgrims liked the name Plymouth. "Maybe our Plymouth will not look much like Plymouth in England," they told each other. "But at least the name will make us think of our homeland."

Captain Jones did his best to sail the *Mayflower* across Cape Cod Bay. He got part way, then had to turn back. Another big storm had come up and he was afraid his ship might be wrecked. The next day it had quieted enough so that they could anchor on the Plymouth side. They were still a long way from shore, as a mile and a half of shallow water lay between them and the beach.

Some of the men again went ashore to look for building sites. A few wanted to put up their houses on the island where they had been forced to take shelter during the first visit. "No one can sneak up and attack us there," they argued. "And look at all those good open fields where we can plant crops."

But more voted in favor of staying on the mainland. "We'll have room to spread out," said one.

"You're right," said another. "We'll never get crowded into the sea here."

"We would have a far better water supply, too," spoke up a third.

After hours of checking back and forth and comparing locations, they finally agreed to build a village near the spot where a large rock broke the smooth sweep of beach. Behind this rock rose a little hill. It led to a still higher hill, which they later named Fort Hill. On one side was a stream, flowing through a deep gully. "This brook will protect us on that side, the hill on another, and the harbor on a third," reasoned Captain Myles Standish. "That leaves just the fourth side to worry about. On that slope we can plant grain. If we build a strong enough fort on top of the hill, I think we would be safe from any attack."

As yet, none of the women or girls had been ashore at Plymouth. One morning, as men and boys were piling into the waiting shallop, the older girls crowded around them. "Can't we go, too?" begged Mary Chilton.

"It is no place for girls, not yet anyway," Governor Carver told them. "And besides, this is much too rough a day for anyone to go ashore who doesn't have to."

He smiled down at them. "I know just how you girls feel, though," he said. "You don't want to be left out of things, do you? Still, I think the most helpful thing you can do right now is to look after Oceanus and Peregrine so their mothers can have a bit of rest. Or see if there is anything you can do for poor Mrs. Allerton, whose baby was born dead yesterday."

On shore the men were working as fast as they could. Some were in the woods chopping trees. Others were stripping them of their branches. After lopping off the branches, still others had to cut the trunks into lumber. They did this by digging a hole in the ground to make a saw pit. One man stood above, one crawled down into the pit. Working together they could pull the saw back and forth to cut boards.

"What hard, backbreaking work this is for men who are weak and sick," said Elder Brewster under his breath. "But we have no time to lose, sick or not sick!"

Before the first day was over, the weary, struggling Pilgrims had wished they had oxen or a horse. But there had been no room to crowd livestock into the *Mayflower*. Some of the men dragged the beams and boards from the saw pit to the spot others had marked out for the first building.

By Christmas Day they had enough lumber to start work on the first house. It was called the Common House and was to be shared by all. First it would be used to store their things, and later it would be a place to hold meetings.

The leaders soon saw that they would never be able to build enough houses for everyone before the *Mayflower* sailed for home. So the single men were told they must scurry around to find a family with whom they could stay for a while.

"If we double up this way, we will need only nineteen houses," Governor Carver explained. "And if we draw lots, nobody will ever be able to say that another grabbed the best place for his home."

All Christmas Day the men on shore worked like beavers.

Some of the Strangers grumbled a bit because it was Christmas. "Christmas is a holiday!" they reminded the leaders.

That was the trouble. Christmas was the most wonderful day of the year for those of the Pilgrims who belonged to the Church of England, but just a day like any other for those who were Separatists. As the Separatists were the ones who had organized the group and were in command, they said that every man must work.

Back on the *Mayflower* some of the women and children were spending an unhappy Christmas, too. Many of the Strangers thought of the good times their friends were having that day in England. They could almost hear the carols being sung from door to door. They could see in their minds' eye the flickering yule logs and the feasting on roast pig or a great side of beef.

"How I wish we were back home in London," whispered some of the homesick women to each other.

The Strangers were not the only ones who missed Christmas. Even some of the little children who had grown up in Holland missed the fun their Dutch playmates would be having at this season. "I wonder what Saint Nicholas and Black Peter brought Jan this year?" six-year-old Wrestling Brewster asked his friend Bartholomew Allerton.

Kind Captain Jones felt sorry for all of them. That evening as he watched them huddled in groups — trying to keep warm in the unheated ship as the storm swirled around them — he wondered what he could do. "This is no place for a

Christmas pageant. And as for bringing in a yule log if we had one — it would just set fire to the ship."

He talked it over with the first mate. "I'm as sick of hardtack and pickled meat as they are," admitted the captain. "But there is no way on earth to get plum pudding or a baby pig to roast out here. What would you think if I offered them some beer?"

The mate agreed. So on Christmas evening Captain Jones broke out a barrel of the precious beer that had been hidden away for the long voyage home.

The flickering light of a tiny fire in one of the sandboxes lit his face as he began to speak. "Everywhere tonight may man have a fire, food, and something to drink," he began. "And may there be rest for the weary and a share in God's blessing for all of us."

Then he took the first drink and invited everyone on board who liked beer to step up and have some too.

10.
Dreadful Winter

As soon as the Common House was finished, the men were able to start work on their own cottages, which would line the road up the hill.

John Alden had arranged to live with the Standish family and to help the captain build his house. They had not known each other before they were hired to go with the group, but they became lifelong friends.

Some days it was so bitter cold that no work at all could be done on the houses. Food was getting scarce as well and every day some of the men had to go in search of game. Some of the boys tried to fish from the *Mayflower*, but they did not have much luck. The Pilgrims had not brought the right kind of fish hooks.

Everybody was suffering from the cold. The only way to stay warm was to snuggle down in the bedclothes. This was all right for small children and babies, but fathers and mothers and the hired hands had to be up and about no matter what the weather.

Already many of the men were too ill to work, sick from the terrible exposure suffered when they were wrecked on Clark's Island. Even some of the small children, who had scarcely set foot off the *Mayflower*, were sick. By Christmas Day six of the passengers were dead. The first child to die was little Jasper More, a London waif who, with his two brothers and his little sister, had been parceled out to several families who had agreed to give them a home in the New World.

Early in January Governor Carver himself became very ill, and a few days later William Bradford collapsed while at work. So many people were now ill that the Common House served as a rough hospital, in addition to a storage shed, and the men were bedded down on the floor.

During this time the roof caught fire and burned off. Carver and Bradford, sick as they were, managed to escape, but they lost most of their things in the blaze.

Most of the winter the women and children continued to live on the ship, which was anchored about a mile and a half off shore. One of those most loved on board was Rose Standish, the military leader's young wife. Her sweet face and gentle manner made her dear to all the Pilgrims. When anyone seemed homesick or lonely, Rose knew how to cheer them. But Rose herself no longer smiled as much as she had when first they landed.

Myles Standish sighed as he watched her grow more weak and pale each day. "My poor little Rose," he whispered. "You are too frail a flower for this wild, rough life."

"Don't worry about me," she would always reply. "I shall be better when I can leave the ship and live in our own house."

But the brave captain trembled with fear as he saw how flushed her face was with fever. He knew an enemy had come that he could not conquer. After a few more days of suffering Myles Standish was left alone.

At last there came a day when only six or seven were well enough to hunt for food, nurse the sick, and bury the dead. Strongest of all were Elder Brewster, the oldest Pilgrim among them, and wiry, redheaded little Myles Standish.

As long as she was able, eighteen-year-old Priscilla Mullins moved quietly about nursing the sick. Then one morning Priscilla could not rise. She, too, was burning with fever. In her illness, she would talk of her home in England. She thought she was a little girl again, playing with her baby brother Joseph. She was too sick to know that during this time her mother and Joseph had both been laid under the snow on the hill where her father had been buried in February. Priscilla was all alone in the world now.

Every few days another Pilgrim would die. Those who were left became afraid to have so many graves showing. They feared the village might be attacked if the Indians knew that there were only a few able-bodied men left. Sometimes they buried the dead in the dark of the night. As soon as the grave was filled, they covered it over with snow. In this way they hoped that the Indians would not see that another grave had been added.

The Pilgrims did not know that by the time the *Mayflower* sailed for England, nearly half their number would lie buried on the hill.

An early spring brought health and hope to the survivors. The sun shone and the birds began to sing in the trees. Axes rang out in the forest as work began again on half-built cottages.

The Pilgrims were puzzled. They had seen some Indians at a distance and had lost some of the tools which they had carelessly left away from camp. But they had not come face to face with a single Indian at Plymouth.

One morning late in March, the men of the colony were holding a meeting in the Common House, talking over plans for their little army with Captain Myles Standish.

"On top of the hill we must build a fort. There

we can mount our own weapons and the ones Captain Jones has given us from the *Mayflower*," Standish was explaining. "If any Indians make trouble, we can bring the women and children into the fort for safety — "

He got no further. A frightened scream from the children at play outside made him pause. The next moment a tall, almost completely naked Indian stood in the door of the Common House. He would have walked right in if the men had not stopped him.

The Indian had long, straight black hair, cut in bangs across the front. He carried a bow.

Every man sprang to his feet and made a dive for sword or gun.

The tall bronze figure did not flinch, although he laid his hand upon a little hatchet at his belt. His sharp, black eyes glanced from face to face.

"Welcome, Englishmen!" he said.

The Pilgrims looked as if they had seen a ghost. An almost naked savage greeting them in their own language!

Myles Standish was the first to recover. "Look to your guns, men," he whispered. "This Indian may not be as friendly as he seems."

Perhaps the Indian heard the captain's words, for he said quickly, "Samoset is friend of Englishmen. Samoset says welcome." William Brewster stepped forward and gave his hand to the strange visitor. "Thank you for your kind words, friend. Where did you learn our language?"

"Samoset is Sagamore of Pemaquid. Many English come in ships to fish and to buy skins."

Then he began to name the captains of some of the ships whose crew had fished near his home, and explained to the Pilgrims how he had sailed down the coast from Maine a few months before with a Captain Dermer, who had visited Cape Cod.

The Pilgrims tossed him a horseman's coat to put on, as it made them shiver to see him standing there without clothing on a windy March day.

All afternoon they talked together. Samoset asked them for beer, but the men explained that they did not have any themselves. They did have some biscuits and butter and cheese from the ship. They gave him these, some pudding, a piece of duck, and something to drink.

Samoset smacked his lips and said that he liked English food.

"Are your friends near here?" asked Myles Standish.

"Always many Indians in forest," answered Samoset. "Indians are good hunters. Get furs. Trade furs. Indians make good traps. English do not."

Many of the Pilgrims looked at Bradford and smiled. They were remembering the Indian deer trap in which he had been caught.

Samoset also cleared up the mystery that had been worrying the Pilgrims ever since they had first seen Plymouth.

He told them that the Patuxet Indians, who had lived there and whose fields they had taken over, were all dead. A great sickness had struck the tribe, killing everyone.

"It must have been the hand of God," said Elder Brewster, "that guided our ships toward Plymouth."

Night came on and still Samoset was in no hurry to leave. He strolled about, peering into cottage doors. He saw that this frightened the women and children — and seemed to enjoy doing it.

"What shall we do with him?" people began to ask each other as bedtime drew near and still Samoset made no move to go. "Perhaps," they thought, "he is a spy sent by neighboring tribes." They were afraid to anger him by sending him away.

Myles Standish had the solution.

"Would you like to sleep on the *Mayflower* tonight?" he asked.

Samoset liked the idea and nodded. They started to row out, but had to turn back, as the wind was too strong.

"He may stay in my house tonight," Stephen Hopkins finally offered. "I believe he is a friendly Indian and will do us no harm."

Mrs. Hopkins did not look pleased, but started

to spread a bed for him on the floor. But Samoset would not sleep the English way. He unrolled a deerskin and curled up on it before the fire. His dark skin glistened in the firelight.

Stephen Hopkins did not sleep. All night long he watched the Indian on his hearth. He had assured the others that Samoset was friendly, and wanted very much to believe it. But still he was afraid to close his eyes for fear he would wake up to find his family dead and his house in flames.

Very few of the Pilgrims slept soundly that night. If they heard an owl hoot or a wolf howl, they thought it was an Indian signal. Every minute they expected Indians to swarm down on the little settlement.

But the night passed without trouble. The next morning Samoset left with a knife, a ring, and a bracelet as presents. He promised to return soon with some of the Wampanoag tribe with whom he was visiting.

"Tell your friends the Wampanoag to bring furs with them and we will buy them," the Pilgrims promised. "But do not bring bows and arrows, knives, or hatchets into Plymouth when you call. This is our law," they warned.

11.
Squanto Tells
His Story

Two days later Samoset was back. This time he brought with him five Wampanoags. They had dressed in their finest clothing to come to the white men's village. Each wore a deerskin over his shoulder, long leather leggings, and a feather in his hair. One had also tied to his head a foxtail that bounced with every step he took.

Their long, straight black hair was cut like Samoset's. Several of them had painted their faces from forehead to chin with a streak the width of four fingers. These streaks were yellow, red, or black — whichever color they liked best against their gleaming copper skin.

"What shall we do, Mother Brewster?" Priscilla Mullins asked the kindly woman who had given the girl a home after her parents and brother died. "Samoset and his friends make six more hungry mouths to feed."

"I am sure we have enough food to share with them," Mrs. Brewster replied. "We can set up a place for them in the Common House, so that they will not have to come to any of the cottages. The children get so frightened when they see them peering in at the doors."

The six Indians had a happy day. They gobbled down as much English food as they could hold and then sang and danced for the Pilgrims — the Indian way of saying "Thank you."

Samoset's friends returned the Pilgrims' tools that had disappeared.

The Wampanoag had also brought furs to trade. They spread them on the floor and then pointed to bowls, pots, and knives that belonged to the Pilgrims. These were things they wanted in exchange.

But the Pilgrim men refused to trade.

"No, Samoset, this is the Sabbath. The Sabbath is the Lord's day, and we cannot trade with you and your friends on the Lord's day," explained Elder Brewster to the puzzled Indians. "If you will come back tomorrow, we will be glad to buy all your furs."

Poor Samoset! He could not understand these strange Englishmen. First they would say yes, then they would say no, to beaverskins! What did they mean by the "Lord's day"? Why was one day any better than another for trading?

He did the best he could to explain what the

Pilgrims had said. The Wampanoag were as puzzled as Samoset by this strange custom of the white men. All they could do was roll up their furs and leave the village. That is, all left but Samoset. He said that he was "too sick" to go.

This frightened the Pilgrims. Was he really sick? Could it be that their English food had not agreed with him? Or could this be part of an Indian plot to keep a spy in their village? Maybe Samoset was not ill at all and was using this as an excuse to stay behind!

Monday — Tuesday — Wednesday dragged slowly by and Samoset was still with them.

Finally the Pilgrim leaders gave him an English hat, a pair of stockings, English shoes, a shirt, and a piece of cloth to wrap around his middle. Decked out in these presents, he was sent to find out why his friends had never come back to sell their furs.

As soon as Samoset had gone, the shallop was dispatched to the *Mayflower* to bring the remaining women and children ashore. For three months Captain Jones had allowed them to live on board while the men were busy on shore building the houses. Now enough houses had been built to shelter everyone, and Captain Jones was anxious to get his ship ready to sail back to England. Myles Standish had called another meeting in the Common House to talk over plans for the fort and to brief each one on what should be done in case of attack. As he was speaking, Francis Billington and Love Brewster rushed in.

"Indians! Indians!" they gasped. "We saw them — hundreds of Indians!"

Myles Standish dashed for the door. The boys were right, there were Indians. But there were only two or possibly three standing on the hill — not hundreds. They were talking together and pointing toward Plymouth village.

With no thought to his own safety, Standish strode toward them, but they slunk away.

The next day was warm and springlike. The men were drilling near the Common House when Indians again appeared. Samoset was returning with four friends. Standish and Edward Winslow went forward to meet them.

"Squanto, friend of English," said Samoset, pointing to one of them.

Squanto told the Pilgrims in broken English that this was his home. He was the only one of his whole tribe, the Patuxet, still alive! And he was alive because he — Squanto — had been in Europe.

He said that he had been one of a group of Indians tricked by a ship's captain and taken to Europe to be sold as slaves. He had escaped and after many adventures managed to reach England. There he had been given a home by a kindly merchant. But he was anxious to get back to his own people, and the merchant had gotten him aboard a ship going to Newfoundland. He had spent much time in Newfoundland and finally got a ride in a ship going down to Maine. From there he had walked. "This place was called Accomack when the Patuxet lived here. Now the Patuxet are all dead. While Squanto was gone, there was a great sickness and the men, women, and children all died."

Squanto's story agreed with what Samoset had told them.

Now the Pilgrims knew why they had found bones of Indians lying on the ground when they arrived. The last Patuxet had died and there was no one left to bury him. This was the reason their exploring party had found deserted cornfields and gardens. This was the reason they had not been attacked in the three months they had been living at Accomack. The Indians whom they had seen or met through Samoset were just curious neighbors — they did not belong here either.

12.
Treaty
with Massasoit

When next they visited Plymouth, Squanto and Samoset had important news. Massasoit, Sachem of the Wampanoag and overlord of all the Indian tribes for many miles around, was on his way to see the Pilgrims.

Squanto and Samoset had a hard time making their new friends understand. By the time the Pilgrim leaders really knew what was meant, Massasoit and his brother Quadequina and about sixty warriors were coming into sight. They advanced as far as the crest of a nearby hill. There they stood, silently waiting and watching.

The Pilgrim men came out from their village. They, too, stood waiting and watching. Both groups were afraid to make the next move.

This was Squanto's great moment. He remembered how some of his friends among the Wampanoag had laughed and said he was only "talking big" when he said that he knew the words of the white man. They had not believed him. Now he would show them!

Squanto slowly walked over to the hill where the Indians were and talked with his "king."

Massasoit told him to go back and tell the Englishmen that he, Massasoit, wanted one of their number to come over to talk with him.

Squanto returned to the little group of worried Pilgrims and delivered Massasoit's message. What a wonderful time he was having! All Indian eyes were upon him; he could feel them boring through his back. This was his big test. He would show them that he was not lying when he said he could talk with the white men.

Governor Carver and Myles Standish spoke in low tones for a minute or two. Others joined in. As Massasoit was the most important Indian in this part of New England, according to both Samoset and Squanto, he must be greeted like royalty. They would give him a king's welcome.

Edward Winslow put on all his armor and pulled his helmet down on his head. Then, taking his sword and some gifts, he marched to Massasoit's hill with Squanto and Samoset.

Winslow carried as gifts an odd assortment of things: a pair of knives, a chain with a bright-colored stone in it, an old earring, a little brandy, some hard ship's biscuit, and a little butter that had been made nine months earlier in England.

Just as if he had been giving a message to the King of France, he bowed and said:

"King James of England sends the King of the Indians a greeting of love and peace. King James accepts Massasoit as his friend and ally. Our Governor Carver, who speaks for King James, would like to talk with Massasoit and would like to make a treaty of peace with him."

Massasoit listened carefully as Squanto and Samoset did the best they could to put the English words into Indian words that Massasoit would understand.

Massasoit seemed to know what they were trying to tell him and nodded his head. He thought it a fitting message for one king to send another.

Next he looked at his gifts and smacked his lips as he chewed the stale biscuits dipped in rancid butter. But the things that struck his fancy most were the corselet, helmet, and sword that Winslow was wearing. If only he could have them! He would trade any number of beaverskins — whatever the man would ask.

Winslow thought fast. He knew he did not dare part with his armor, but at the same time he could not afford to make Massasoit angry. And so he made his face as long and sad as possible and replied, "I am sorry that I cannot trade, not for all the beaverskins in the world. My King would be angry. I must obey my King."

Massasoit understood. He knew that men must

obey their king's wishes, even if the king is across the ocean.

After further talk it was agreed that Winslow would stay with Quadequina and some of the band, while Massasoit and about twenty of his finest men would go over to call on the Pilgrims.

The Indians towered over most of the English, who looked pale and puny in comparison. Massasoit and his guard were handsome and well formed. They were all dressed alike except for an important-looking necklace of white bone beads that the leader wore.

All were naked except for moccasins and loin cloths. Each had a feather in his hair, a thick coating of grease smeared over his skin, and streaks of red, black, white, or yellow paint daubed on his face. Massasoit had chosen a deep mulberry red.

Myles Standish and an officer visiting from the *Mayflower* took six men and advanced to meet the Indian party at the brook. They walked with them from that point to one of the half-finished houses. While this was taking place, other Pilgrims worked fast to prepare a "throne room." They spread a green blanket on the floor and placed several bright cushions on it for the honored guest and for Governor Carver to sit on.

As soon as Massasoit had been seated and his guard had taken their places about the room, a drum and trumpet announced, as loudly as possible, the arrival of Governor Carver. He was decked out in the finest clothing the Pilgrim band could find, and wore his full armor.

Governor Carver kissed Massasoit's hand.

Massasoit kissed him in return.

Both men then sat down on the green blanket, and Governor Carver offered Massasoit something to eat and drink. Massasoit shared the food with his men and then reached up and took some tobacco from a little bag around his neck and offered it to Carver. As they smoked, the two leaders worked out a treaty:

Massasoit promised that the Wampanoag and the other tribes that were subject to him would not hurt the Pilgrims; or if any of them did, Massasoit would send the guilty Indian to the Pilgrims to be punished.

The Pilgrims promised that if any of their people injured the Indians, they would do the same.

Next, Massasoit promised that if any Indians took the Pilgrims' tools or other things belonging to the Pilgrims, Massasoit would see that they were returned. The Pilgrims promised to do the same.

Both leaders promised that their people would help the other if attacked. Massasoit also promised to let all the other Indian tribes in the vicinity know that he and the Pilgrims were now allies.

Both leaders agreed that when they or any of their people visited the other, they would arrive without weapons.

Finally, the English promised Massasoit that King James of England accepted Massasoit as his friend and ally.

When Massasoit returned to the rest of his group, the Pilgrims asked a few of his men to remain as hostages until Winslow got back to them. The Pilgrims thought this would take only a few minutes. Instead, much to their surprise, Quadequina, Massasoit's brother, now wanted to visit Plymouth and taste their food. And so the whole long "royal welcome" had to be repeated!

Massasoit and the Pilgrim leaders meant what they said when they promised to be friends for the rest of their lives. But no one would have believed that day that the treaty "talked out" by the two men sitting on cushions on a green blanket would last for more than fifty years.

13.
On Their Own

A few days later Priscilla Mullins and Mary Chilton were poking through the dead leaves to see if any wild flowers were starting to bloom. With them was little Mary Allerton, whose mother had died. The older girls were taking care of her.

"I wish we could find a few flowers to give Mistress Brewster for her birthday," said Priscilla.

"Maybe it is too early for violets over here," replied her friend. "See, there is still a pocket of snow in this hollow."

"Let's take her this," Mary Allerton piped up. The child had dropped to her knees and was busily digging up a furry-stemmed hepatica plant, now often called "May flower."

"Mary is right," thought Priscilla. "Maybe this isn't as pretty as tulips or roses or violets would be, but Mistress Brewster will like it anyway."

As the three girls came out of the clearing, they glanced across the water of Plymouth Bay toward the *Mayflower*, still anchored a mile and a half away. The ship seemed almost like home to them.

The sailors on board had hated most of the passengers and had made their lives miserable. Still the Pilgrims were going to miss the ship. She would be sailing for home any day now. The winter storms were past and with the crew now well enough to work, the captain wanted to get started.

The next day a meeting was called in the Common House. Everybody who could was asked to report. Captain Jones had something he wanted to talk over with them.

The Pilgrims were going to miss Captain Jones. He had been good to them. He had not dumped them ashore and sailed away with winter coming on, as many ship captains would have done. Instead, he had stood by until they got settled, letting the weaker ones live on the ship all winter.

He had shared with them when they ran short. He had given them cannon from the *Mayflower* that he might need for his own protection against pirates on the way home, and had even helped them get the guns ashore and mounted.

There was a hushed silence in the Common House when the *Mayflower*'s captain began to speak.

"Tomorrow if we get a fair wind, we plan to set

sail," he began. "The ship is almost ready. If need be, we could leave in a few hours."

Slowly his eyes traveled around the group. He saw how pale and thin and woebegone they all looked. He was worried. His eyes, which could flash like steel when he was giving orders on the *Mayflower*, softened as he looked down at all the Pilgrim children.

"Why, half this colony is now under sixteen years of age!" he thought to himself as he glanced from face to face.

It was true. Only four of the mothers were still alive. Already nearly half the men were gone — and those some of the strongest and youngest.

Even whole families were missing. The Martins, the Tinkers, the Turners, and the Rigdales were all dead.

The captain's glance rested on Baby Eaton, curled up on Mrs. Brewster's lap. Big eyes in his pointed little face made him look like a hungry baby robin. Captain Jones could remember how happy the child had looked the first time he had seen him — a chubby, cooing baby in his mother's arms. Now his mother was dead — and anybody who had a free moment looked after the little Eaton.

"We have all had a long, hard, and very sad winter," Captain Jones continued. "You have laid half your number on the hill, and I have lost many of my men. Perhaps it would be the wise thing for you to give up and return with me to England. I will take you back."

The Pilgrims thought of the loved ones they had buried. Hardly a family had been spared at least one death. But if they gave up now and returned, the ones who had lost their lives would have died in vain.

Those who had left wives or children in England or Holland thought of them.

Mrs. Brewster's eyes filled with tears when she thought of Jonathan and the girls, Fear and Patience, who had been left behind in Leyden. Should she return to them? This might be the last chance she would ever have to see them again.

"No," she thought. "I shall stay. Sometime they will all be able to come to us here."

The captain's eyes turned toward the Billingtons. He knew that the Billington family did not get along well with the others. He knew that nearly every family on board considered them loud mouthed and good for nothing. Maybe they would welcome a chance to get back to London.

John Billington's wife glanced toward her two boys as if she were reading the captain's mind.

"I know we are not much," her eyes seemed to say, "but maybe Francis and John will amount to something here."

William Bradford was the first to speak aloud. He was still weak from the illness that had almost cost his life.

"Friends, we have all heard the captain's kind offer," he began. "What do you say? Are there any here among us who would like to go back to England with him? Speak up!"

There was complete silence.

The captain tried again. Seeing how frail and unhappy they all looked, he asked, "Is there not one of you who would like to return?"

"No!" came the answer. "Our homes are here now. And here we stay!"

"But how about the young girls who have lost everybody in their family?" the captain of the *Mayflower* persisted. "Wouldn't they like me to take them back to their relatives?"

"Speak up, Priscilla," Governor Carver urged the only survivor of the Mullins family.

"I have no home to go to other than the one that Elder Brewster and his family have offered me," said Priscilla.

"And how about you?" said Governor Carver, turning to Mary Chilton.

"I have no wish to go back to England either, since all I have is here in Plymouth," said Mary.

"Humility Cooper and I are not returning either," spoke up Elizabeth Tilley.

Governor Carver looked at the girls. "Do not answer in haste," he warned. "Think what it will mean to stay in this wild new land."

Then, turning to the heads of families he said,

"Let each man answer for himself and his family. What say you, Allerton?"

"The Allerton family will stay!"

Governor Carver went on down the list, asking each in turn the same question. Not one of the Pilgrims would accept Captain Jones's kind offer.

14.
Squanto Helps
the Pilgrims

When Massasoit and Quadequina returned to their homes, Squanto did not go with them. He wanted to stay with the Pilgrims.

He helped them in many ways. He knew every path in the forest and guided them when they went hunting. He knew just where the deer went to drink at night and at dawn, and showed the Pilgrims how to make deer traps near the brooks. He bent down strong branches and fastened them to the ground. When the deer stepped on the tip of a branch, its foot would be caught in a snare and the branch would fly up, carrying the helpless animal with it.

"A cruel trap, Squanto," William Bradford told him, remembering how he had once been caught in just such a deer trap and had been left dangling by one leg. "We must never use it if we can get food in any other way."

"Yes, better to shoot deer, but Indians have no gun."

Squanto could move through the forest without breaking a twig or causing even one dry leaf to rustle. He could lie on the ground or wriggle through tall grass without being seen. He knew how to make a trap of willow twigs to catch fish in the brook, how to make a bear trap of logs, and how to call the wild ducks.

He knew which berries were good to eat and which ones were poison. He showed them a small trailing plant that grew in mossy salt marshes and had pale yellow berries which would later turn red. The Indians called them "cran berries" or "crane berries," because, when in blossom, they looked like the head of a crane. They were also called "bear berries," because bears liked them.

Squanto showed the Pilgrim women how the Indians cooked. He taught them to make *Nokake*, which every Indian on the march carried with him in a little basket at his back. A pinch of this meal and a little water would keep them going.

Squanto parched the kernels of dried corn, which all the Indians stored underground in big baskets like the ones that the first *Mayflower* exploring parties had dug up at Cornhill. When browned, the kernels were ground with a mortar and pestle. The Indians used a pole, pounding in a hole hollowed from a log.

Squanto knew how to "tread out" eels by wading into streams at certain places. He knew how to lay a stone "nest" on the sand to start an Indian clambake.

He taught the Pilgrims how to build a fire on top of these stones to make them sizzling hot. Then he would rake the embers aside and spread a layer of rockweed over the hot stones, then a layer of clams, then another layer of the weed. Over this heap of stones, clams, and rockweed Squanto placed green branches or whatever he could find that would hold the heat in so it would steam the clams.

It was hard for the Pilgrims to eat the clams, oysters, scallops, and sea snails that the Indians liked. But they thought the eels delicious.

When nearby Indians came to trade, Squanto helped the Pilgrims. Only he could tell each side what the other group was saying.

"How could we ever talk to our neighbors if anything happened to Squanto?" thought Edward Winslow not long after Squanto came to live with the Pilgrims. "I think I will try to learn the Indian language while Squanto is here to teach me."

So Squanto became Winslow's teacher, and when they were alone they would use the Indian language. This made Squanto very happy.

Squanto wanted to learn to read a book. "Show Squanto how to make paper talk?" he begged Winslow one day.

A book seemed almost magic to Squanto. He

called it a "speaking paper." Indians sometimes wrote messages with paint on a great flat rock or with a bit of charcoal on bark, but their writing was in pictures. They had nothing like the tiny squiggles that the white man could put on paper to make it "talk."

There were no primers, so Winslow took out his Bible. It was the book from which he had learned to read; he would teach Squanto from it.

One day Squanto came in from the woods, carrying a little oak branch in his hand. Pointing to its tiny leaves he said, "See! Oak leaves are big as mouse's ear. Time to plant corn now."

Then he went down to the brook and set a net to catch the alewives — a kind of herring — as they swam up the stream to spawn.

Next morning Governor Carver met him coming from the brook with a basket of the fish.

"Why Squanto!" he exclaimed. "What are you going to do with those? They seem much too small to eat."

"Indian plant corn here many times," answered Squanto. "Now ground hungry, too."

Squanto had the Pilgrims plant corn in the Indian way. They went into the old Indian fields, which were now choked with weeds, since no crop had been grown in the years since the Patuxet had died. The Indian showed the Pilgrims how to pull up the weeds and dig holes about four feet apart, loosening the earth with a pointed stick.

Everybody had to work — men, boys, girls, and small children. Thousands of holes must be dug on the twenty acres in which they wanted to plant Indian corn the first year. Then still more thousands of alewives had to be trapped in the brook, dragged in baskets up its steep banks and into the fields for fertilizer.

Even the youngest could help. Squanto showed them how to place in each hole three of the herring with heads together like the spokes of a wheel, and then drop seeds on top of the fish. Squanto showed the children how to count out beans, kernels of corn, and squash seeds for each hole — making a little game of it.

"Why do we have to do what an old Indian says?" whined Francis Billington.

"All seeds hungry. Ground hungry. Corn, beans, squash, ground — all eat fish!" was Squanto's slow answer when he heard the boy. He tried to say more but could not find words in English to tell the children all the Indians knew about farming.

The backbreaking work in the cornfields, planting thousands and thousands of hills of corn by hand, proved too much for Governor Carver. One day his head ached so that he had to leave the field to lie down. It was too late; within a few days he died without being conscious again.

William Bradford was then elected governor.

15.
Visit
to Massasoit

When summer came, the Pilgrims knew that they had chosen a good place to live. Green hills and fields, bright flowers, birds singing in the treetops — how different Plymouth looked in the warm sunshine from the Plymouth they had known the first winter.

Warm weather and sunshine seemed to bring Indians. Not just one or two but dozens, who came to visit and be fed. They came to the shore for lobster and fish, and while there took time out to visit their new English neighbors.

The Pilgrims tried to treat them kindly and gave them food. This wonderful news spread far and wide so that more and more Indian "tourists" dropped in to get acquainted — and always stayed to be fed.

Finally, Pilgrim leaders grew desperate. There were so many Indian visitors camped around that it was hard to get needed work done. They did not want to seem stingy. And they certainly did not want to do anything that would offend Massasoit or any of his people. But they could not go on keeping "open house" forever.

They decided this might be a good time to send some men to pay back Massasoit's visit to them, and to ask his help in solving the problem. And while they were there, they could also ask his help in finding the Indians whom they owed for the corn they had dug up on Cape Cod.

Edward Winslow and Stephen Hopkins were chosen to make the trip. Squanto made a third, as he was to be their guide. They carried presents for the Sagamore: a red horseman's coat and a copper chain.

They arrived at Sowams, the village about forty miles from Plymouth where Massasoit made his headquarters. He was not at home.

Word was sent to him that important visitors were waiting for him and he soon arrived to give them a warm welcome.

Winslow and Hopkins presented the red coat. Massasoit admired the color and put it right on.

Then Winslow and Hopkins delivered their message. They told him how happy everyone in Plymouth was to have his people visit them, but they were short of food to feed so many. They hated to ask this of their honored friend and ally, but would Massasoit be willing to ask his people not to come to Plymouth unless they had skins to trade or came with a message from him?

They were quick to add that they would always — at all times — be glad to see Massasoit himself or his own personal friends — but they could not keep "open house" any longer for every one of his people.

"So that we shall know that a messenger really comes from you," Winslow said in handing him the copper chain, "have him bring this chain that we are giving you. If an Indian is wearing this chain, we will know he comes from you."

Then they asked Massasoit to help them find the owners of the corn they had stolen so they could pay for it.

Business was now finished and Massasoit lighted tobacco and gave some to his guests. Alas, Massasoit knew all too well what the Pilgrims meant when they said they had little to feed guests.

Massasoit was short of food, too. He had nothing to offer Winslow or Hopkins for supper. When they saw that they were not going to be fed, the Pilgrims said that they were so tired they would like to rest.

The best that Massasoit could offer them was a place on one end of his own bed — a row of planks set about a foot from the ground and covered with a thin pad.

The next noon Massasoit had two fish for dinner. They were fine fresh fish. The only trouble was that they had to be shared by forty people.

The following day Winslow and Hopkins insisted they had to start home. They felt sorry for Massasoit. They knew it hurt him to have them see how poor he was. But they were getting so weak with loss of sleep and only one meal in thirty-six hours that they could hardly stand.

"Why, what's the matter?" children rushed forward to ask as the two men staggered into Plymouth five days after they had left.

"Matter!" roared Hopkins. "We are starving, that is all that is the matter! You try to live five days on a few nuts and a bite of fish and you would stagger, too."

"To say nothing of sleeping six to a bed — not counting the lice, fleas, and mosquitoes!" added Winslow, scratching himself.

Not long after the visit to Massasoit's camp, a second Indian decided to make his home with the Pilgrims. He was not like Squanto, a man who had lost all his people. Hobomok, as he was called, was one of Massasoit's important warriors.

16.
First Harvest

The days and weeks passed quickly during the summer of 1621, and soon it was autumn. On the whole, the crops had been good. Only the peas were a disappointment. The seed brought from England came up and blossomed. Then the hot New England sun burned the vines so that no pods were filled.

The barley had done fairly well, and the corn crop was excellent. The corn had been cut and stacked for drying in the way the Indians had taught them. Fishing had been successful, too. There were bass and cod for each family to share, and there were plenty of wild turkey, ducks, and geese. With luck there would be venison.

Seven houses and four public buildings had been completed.

The Pilgrims were happy that things were

going so well; it looked as if they were over their worst troubles.

During October, the most beautiful season of all in New England, the leaves turned a brilliant red and yellow and the weather strangely became milder than it had been a few weeks before. Day after day the sky remained a rich, bright blue.

"To think we could have known weather like this last year if we had not had so much trouble with the *Speedwell*," ran through Pilgrim minds. "What a difference it would have made in our lives if we had arrived even a month or two earlier!"

The Pilgrims were not the only ones enjoying the lovely fall weather. One morning guests arrived — Massasoit and ninety of his people. They had come for a three-day visit.

Nice weather, plenty to eat, and good friends — what more was needed to have a feast?

But the first roll of the drum called all to prayers.

"The white men talk to the Great Spirit," Squanto explained.

"They thank him for his good gifts," added Hobomok.

The Indians seemed to understand and listened quietly to the prayers. Then there was food for all: clams, eels, corn bread, dried fruit, leeks, watercress, plums, roast duck and goose, and bowls of pudding made from Indian corn. This was a picnic or cookout. No building in Plymouth could hold 140 people celebrating.

After everyone had eaten, Governor Bradford led the men to a grassy spot where they could play games. The Indians astonished their hosts by the great skill they showed in running and jumping.

After the Indians had performed for the white men, Governor Bradford asked them to sit on the grass and watch the Pilgrim soldiers drill. The Indians sat down, not knowing what to expect next.

Suddenly they were startled by the sound of a trumpet and the roll of the drum. Down the slope marched the little Pilgrim "army" — less than twenty men! To the right and left they wheeled, in single file and in pairs. At a word from Captain Myles Standish every man suddenly fired his musket in the air.

This was not at all what the Indians were expecting and a few sprang to their feet in alarm. Again came the sharp report of the guns. The Indians were still more alarmed.

"These men are our friends; they will not harm us," Massasoit insisted.

Hardly had he finished speaking when there came a roar from the cannon. The sound echoed from hill to hill. At this the Indians became badly alarmed. They did not like the Pilgrims' way of having a party.

Some thought of an excuse to get away.

"We must go into the forest and hunt," they told everyone. "We must get deer for the feast."

Captain Standish smiled as he saw the Indians start for the forest. "They do not like the thunder of our cannon."

But the next day the five Indians did come back, each one dragging a fine deer.

This made the greatest feast of all. Everyone was busy dressing the game, piling wood on the fire, barbecuing the meat. Never had the Indians seen so many good things to eat at one time. How the Great Spirit must love his white children!

On the third day the Indians moved on and the Pilgrims took stock of what they had left. "If we are careful, we will have enough to last the winter out," they thought.

17.
Arrival
of the *Fortune*

Governor Bradford and Edward Winslow were walking along the crest of a hill one morning in November. They had their guns and several ducks they had just shot.

Suddenly they heard a light, quick step on the dry leaves behind them. An Indian was running toward them. He pointed toward the sea and tried his best to tell them something, but couldn't make them understand.

"We had better get Squanto," said Bradford.

"Indian says a great ship is coming," Squanto explained. "He says it is already near. He thinks it is a French ship."

Governor Bradford looked troubled. The French were not friendly toward the English. If a French ship came to Plymouth, he knew that it would try to capture the village.

The governor asked Squanto to thank the Indian for warning them of the danger and told him to see that he received food and a gift.

Soon everyone in Plymouth had heard the news, and a cannon was fired as a warning signal to call home all who were off hunting or fishing.

The Pilgrims had not long to wait before a faint speck of sail appeared. It looked as if it were heading straight for Plymouth harbor.

Myles Standish aimed a cannon at the oncoming vessel. "If it is an enemy ship, we must be ready for them," he said. "Every man and boy take a gun or sword or knife."

As the ship grew nearer, the waiting Pilgrims became more and more excited. Hardly a word was spoken, but their white faces showed how anxious they felt. They strained their eyes to see what flag floated from the ship's mast. In every heart was the prayer that it might be a ship from home.

Nearer and nearer it came. All eyes were fixed on the masthead. Now a flash of white could be seen. But what were the darker colors?

"It is an English ship, thank God!"

"An English ship!" The hills rang with their joyful shouts. Priscilla darted from her lookout on the hill to tell Mrs. Brewster the good news. One glance at Priscilla's face was all she needed.

Children who, a few minutes before, had huddled close to the women, now ran up and down the beach shouting.

"I hope my brother Jonathan is on that ship," screamed Love Brewster, hopping first on one foot and then the other.

"I hope that old boat brings the cow we left at home so we can have some butter and cheese," burst out Giles Hopkins. "I'm tired of what we have to eat."

"Be glad you have beans and bread, Giles," said Priscilla, coming up behind him. "Elder Brewster says there is hardly enough corn to last us through the winter, since the Indians feasted so long with us. What we should all be praying is that the ship is bringing us more supplies."

The tiny ship was the *Fortune* of London, only a third the size of the *Mayflower*. A boat was lowered and people began to climb down. Nobody on shore could tell who they were at such a distance.

Some of the Pilgrims were expecting brothers. Some were hoping that sons or daughters or friends might be on board. It seemed to those waiting that the sailors rowed more slowly than ever men had rowed before. Almost the first to touch land was Elder Brewster's son Jonathan. Love Brewster had his wish!

Thirty-five passengers had come to join the colony, but only twelve of them had come from Leyden. All the rest were Strangers, who had been recruited by Weston and the other merchant adventurers.

But whether they were friends or strangers, it was good to hear news from home. It was just a year to the day since those on the *Mayflower* had first seen Cape Cod. In all these months they had not heard from those left behind.

That night Pilgrims sat around a blazing fire in every cottage listening to stories of England and Holland. At Elder Brewster's, Jonathan had much to tell of what he and Patience and Fear had been doing since the *Speedwell* had sailed. He brought many messages from friends at the Green Gate and from their Dutch neighbors.

There was bad news, too.

A letter from Thomas Weston addressed to Governor Carver, who had been dead since April, demanded that they pay their debt to him and angrily complained that the *Mayflower* had returned in the spring without a cargo.

Hurt by Weston's cruel words, the Pilgrims worked desperately the two weeks the *Fortune* stayed at Plymouth to load the ship. They stowed her with clapboard, which brought a very high price in England, and added two hogsheads of beaver and otter skins, which they had traded from the Indians.

This cargo was equal to about half the money the Pilgrims owed the London businessman.

"If we can get another load like this off to them, we shall be free of debt," they rejoiced.

The *Fortune*, filled with her treasure in clapboard and furs and with thirteen people on board, had almost reached England when French pirates seized her. The pirates took everything — clothes, food, equipment, and cargo. The clapboard and the beaver and otter skins that the Pilgrims had worked so hard to send back to pay off their debts were all stolen! And so they had to begin all over again.

A second piece of bad news was the discovery that the thirty-five new colonists had come with nothing at all except the clothing on their backs. They had brought no food to live on until the next harvest; no clothing to wear in winter; no bedding, or equipment, or household goods. They had carried scarcely enough food on the ship to last until they reached Plymouth, and the Pilgrims found that they would have to give the ship corn for the return trip so that those on board would not starve.

Governor Bradford called a meeting of the *Mayflower* Pilgrims. He had to put the facts before them.

"A greater problem now faces us than any we have met before," he told them. "Only a few weeks ago we felt that our harvest had been good and would tide us over the winter. Now we have learned that instead of about fifty mouths to feed, we shall have eighty-five. Food that would have kept fifty in comfort will scarcely keep eighty-five alive until the next harvest."

Men began to stir uneasily as Bradford continued. "It was wicked to send all these people to us without anything to help them make a living. How can they plant crops without seeds or tools? Or cut lumber without axes? Perhaps Weston thinks they can live without food or homes!"

"We shall have to share our own crusts," said Elder Brewster gravely.

"But," demanded Isaac Allerton, "can we share crusts that we don't have? Do we have to starve so that they can eat?"

"Somehow we shall manage if we are all willing to make sacrifices," replied Governor Bradford. "God has kept watch over us so far and He will not desert us now."

History has shown that the Pilgrim leaders had good reason to be fearful. Before the next harvest was gathered, everyone in the colony knew what starvation was like. The men staggered with weakness as they tried to keep at their jobs. Their clothing hung on them in tatters, like rags on a scarecrow. But somehow the Pilgrims managed to survive. They planted crops and built more homes and gradually, as time went on, life became easier in Plymouth.

The children of the *Mayflower* grew up. They married and had children of their own, and then grandchildren and great-grandchildren.

As the years went by, their descendants fanned

out from New England, pushing first into the Middle West and then on toward the Pacific. Today there is scarcely a city in the United States that does not have at least one person whose ancestors came on the *Mayflower*.

Boys and Girls
on the *Mayflower*

Because we often use the words "Pilgrim Fathers," many people think that those who came on the *Mayflower* were old men and women. This was not true. William Brewster, oldest of all the Pilgrims, was under fifty-five. Most of the adults were in their twenties and thirties. About a third of all passengers on the *Mayflower* were children. About half of all who survived the first year were under sixteen.

There were no birth certificates and so it is hard to know exact ages. The best that can be done is to guess — using as clues everything written about the Pilgrims at that time or soon after.

The twenty-seven boys and girls who lived through the first year were:

Name	Probable Age When on the MAYFLOWER
Bartholomew Allerton	8
Mary Allerton	4
Remember Allerton (a girl)	6
Francis Billington	11–13
John Billington, Jr.	14–15
Love Brewster	9
Wrestling Brewster	6
Carver maid (name unknown)	17–18
Mary Chilton	15
John Cooke	12–13
Humility Cooper (a girl)	8–14
John Crackston	10–15
Samuel Eaton (a nursing baby)	½–1
Samuel Fuller, 2nd	4–8
Constance Hopkins	14–15
Damaris Hopkins	3
Giles Hopkins	12–13
Oceanus Hopkins	(born on the *Mayflower* at sea)
William Latham	12–15
Desire Minter	18
Richard More	6–14
Priscilla Mullins	18
Joseph Rogers	14–15
Henry Sampson	6

Elizabeth Tilley	13–15
Peregrine White	(born on the *Mayflower* at Cape Cod)
Resolved White (a boy)	5

There were also nine boys and girls who died during the first year. Not much is known about any of them.

Allerton baby (born dead on the *Mayflower*)

John Hooke (a young boy who came as one of the Allerton servants)

Ellen and Jasper More and a brother whose name is not known (they were three of the four little orphans between six and fourteen, whom Thomas Weston had placed with various families on the *Mayflower*)

Joseph Mullins (probably about six years old)

_____Tinker (age and first name not known)

_____Turner (age and first name not known)

_____Turner (age and first name not known)

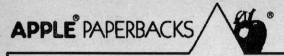

APPLE® PAPERBACKS

Pick an Apple and Polish Off Some Great Reading!

BEST-SELLING APPLE TITLES

❑ MT43944-8	**Afternoon of the Elves** Janet Taylor Lisle	$2.75
❑ MT43109-9	**Boys Are Yucko** Anna Grossnickle Hines	$2.75
❑ MT43473-X	**The Broccoli Tapes** Jan Slepian	$2.95
❑ MT42709-1	**Christina's Ghost** Betty Ren Wright	$2.75
❑ MT43461-6	**The Dollhouse Murders** Betty Ren Wright	$2.75
❑ MT43444-6	**Ghosts Beneath Our Feet** Betty Ren Wright	$2.75
❑ MT44351-8	**Help! I'm a Prisoner in the Library** Eth Clifford	$2.75
❑ MT44567-7	**Leah's Song** Eth Clifford	$2.75
❑ MT43618-X	**Me and Katie (The Pest)** Ann M. Martin	$2.75
❑ MT41529-8	**My Sister, The Creep** Candice F. Ransom	$2.75
❑ MT42883-7	**Sixth Grade Can Really Kill You** Barthe DeClements	$2.75
❑ MT40409-1	**Sixth Grade Secrets** Louis Sachar	$2.75
❑ MT42882-9	**Sixth Grade Sleepover** Eve Bunting	$2.75
❑ MT41732-0	**Too Many Murphys** Colleen O'Shaughnessy McKenna	$2.75

Available wherever you buy books, or use this order form.

Scholastic Inc., P.O. Box 7502, 2931 East McCarty Street, Jefferson City, MO 65102

Please send me the books I have checked above. I am enclosing $_____ (please add $2.00 to cover shipping and handling). Send check or money order — no cash or C.O.D.s please.

Name _____

Address _____

City_____ State/Zip _____

Please allow four to six weeks for delivery. Offer good in the U.S.A. only. Sorry, mail orders are not available to residents of Canada. Prices subject to change.

APP591